My plan is simple.

I am going to take
over the world.

Mr. Penguin's adventures began in

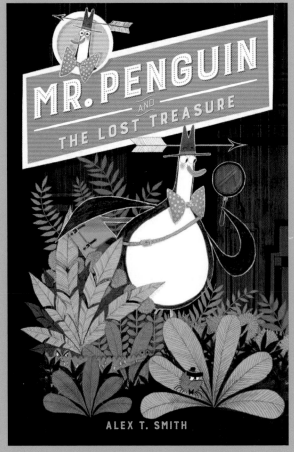

MR. PENGUIN AND **THE LOST TREASURE**

ALEX T. SMITH

HC: $16.95 / 978-1-68263-120-1

★ "Lighthearted and humorous."
—*Booklist*

MR. PENGUIN AND THE FORTRESS OF SECRETS

ALEX T. SMITH

Ω
PEACHTREE
ATLANTA

Mr. Penguin is a penguin.

If you aren't sure whether he is one or not,
all you have to do is look at him.
Here he is now.

He *looks* like a penguin.

He is all black and white with a little beak
and two flappy flippers. When he walks, his
bottom wiggles about in *exactly* the sort of
way a penguin's bottom *should* wiggle.
But there's something rather unusual about
Mr. Penguin. You see, he isn't
JUST a penguin.

He is an *Adventurer!*

He has a dashing hat, an enormous magnifying glass, and a battered satchel—with a nice packed lunch of fish finger sandwiches.

Mr. Penguin's best friend is this spider. His name is Colin. He's really good at kung fu, so you'd better watch out! KAPOW!

That woman with the glasses—she's called Edith Hedge. She's Mr. Penguin's other best friend. The pigeon on her head is Gordon. He doesn't say much.

Together, they've already been on an adventure called *Mr. Penguin and the Lost Treasure*. Are you ready to join them on another?

For Matthew Davidson, Adventurer (and Chum)

Published by
PEACHTREE PUBLISHING COMPANY INC.
1700 Chattahoochee Avenue
Atlanta, Georgia 30318-2112
www.peachtree-online.com

First published in Great Britain in 2018 by Hodder and Stoughton
First United States version published in 2019 by Peachtree Publishing Company Inc.

Artwork created digitally

Printed in April 2019 in China
10 9 8 7 6 5 4 3 2 1
First Edition
ISBN: 978-1-68263-130-0

Library of Congress Cataloging-in-Publication Data

Names: Smith, Alex T., author.
Title: Mr. Penguin and the fortress of secrets / Alex T. Smith.
Description: First edition. | Atlanta : Peachtree Publishing Company Inc., 2019. |
"First published in Great Britain in 2018 by Hodder Children's Books." |
Summary: Aspiring Professional Adventurer Mr. Penguin, his colleague,
Colin the spider, and friends Edith and Gordon crash-land on a snowy mountain
where they face an evil hypnotist and seek missing pets.
Identifiers: LCCN 2018061606 | ISBN 9781682631300
Subjects: | CYAC: Lost and found possessions—Fiction. | Pets—Fiction. |
Hypnotism—Fiction. | Adventure and adventurers—Fiction. | Penguins—Fiction. |
Spiders—Fiction. | Mystery and detective stories.
Classification: LCC PZ7.S6422 Mm 2019 | DDC [Fic]—dc23
LC record available at *https://lccn.loc.gov/2018061606*

CONTENTS

Mr. Penguin's home-and-office—an igloo between two enormous skyscrapers in Cityville—is in darkness.

All is still. The swivel chair behind the desk is empty. A cloth is draped neatly over the typewriter.

And Mr. Penguin's special hat is not hanging on the coat rack as usual. In fact, it's not there at all.

The only sound is the low humming of the refrigerator.

On the mat by the front door, unopened mail is piling up.

On top of the little hill of mail is a letter. It is neatly addressed, and the stamp (from a very faraway place) is stuck down, next to the words AIR MAIL. Inside, the letter says...

Frau Strudel's Haus of Strudel
No. 9 The Town Square
Schneedorf-on-the-Peak
Schneedorf

Dear Mr. Penguin,

My name is Dieter Strudel. I live up on a mountain, and I can't find my hamster.

Actually, quite a lot of rodent pets have gone missing recently, and there are loads of other strange things going on here too.

I've read about your adventures in the newspaper, and I think you might be just the penguin to help me. I know you and your friend Colin are good at solving mysteries.

I don't have much money in my piggy bank, but my mum runs the bakery here so you can have as many cakes as you can eat.

Please come and help me. I really miss Colonel Tuftybum (my hamster).

Yours hopefully,
Dieter Strudel

But Mr. Penguin hasn't read the letter yet, because Mr. Penguin isn't at home. Where on EARTH can he be…?

A DARK AND SHADOWY DEAL

– 6000 MILES FROM CITYVILLE –

GOLDEN
PAGODA HOTEL
金塔酒店

The outdoor ballroom was swarming. On the roof of the luxurious Golden Pagoda Hotel, glamorous couples pranced around the dance floor in the hot, sticky, jasmine-scented night air.

Framed by a pair of spangly curtains, a live band was on the stage. They honked and parped their way through a medley of jazzy hits. Immaculately dressed waiters fluttered about like hummingbirds, topping up glasses with fizzy champagne. Corks popped, bamboo swayed, and hoots of laughter filled the air.

Everyone was having a wonderful time.

Well, almost everyone.

In a dark and shadowy corner, a dark and shadowy deal was being done. A small, scrawny man with a face like a cross-eyed rat was sitting at a table. Beads of sweat ran down his nose. Two enormous men sat opposite him, their faces disappearing off into the gloom. Between them was a

very glamorous lady, tiny compared to her bodyguards and dressed elegantly in a black frock. A small silver brooch by her shoulder—a circle containing an eye—twinkled in the candlelight. When she spoke she smiled, but it didn't quite reach her eyes.

"Do you have it?" she hissed in a dangerous sort of voice.

The ratty man nodded. He was so nervous, the ends of his wispy mustache wobbled about like worried whiskers. Carefully, he lifted a bundle of rags onto the table and started to unroll it. The lady's eyes glinted greedily when the object inside was revealed. She nodded to the giant bodyguard on her left. He extended a hand the size of a tea tray and took the treasure with one swipe, placing it delicately into a padded briefcase and clicking it decisively shut.

Meanwhile, the other body-guard had taken out a huge pile of money from inside his jacket and placed it on the table.

The ratty man didn't wait to be told to take the cash. With shaking hands, he grabbed the money and shoved it frantically down the front of his trousers. Then he gave a curt nod, wove his way through the crowded dance floor, and slid down the back stairs into the night.

He did not look back.

The lady in black watched him leave, like a cat watching a mouse. Then she gathered her fur stole about her shoulders, stood up, and stalked across the crowded room, followed by her bodyguards.

What she and her assistants didn't know was that two beady eyes were watching her make her escape. The beady eyes belonged to the conductor of the band, peering out over the top of his music stand. He had been watching them VERY carefully.

Now, let's just stop and have a good look at this man.

Let's really squint at him…

Hang on!

I...I think that small and rather round little man might not actually be a man at all!

I think he might be a...a...penguin!

A PENGUIN IN DISGUISE!

Yes, he's squeezed into a smart white dinner jacket with a jazzy bow tie, and he has neatly shingled hair. (It's a wig, I'm sure of it!) But beneath all that, he is *definitely* a penguin! The beak, despite the fake mustache stuck to the end of it, is a dead giveaway. It's Mr. Penguin!

Let's see what he's up to...

Mr. Penguin watched the lady and her bodyguards snake across the dance floor.

He narrowed his eyes.

Judging the moment just right, he raised his baton, and at a flick of his flipper, the band started to play again. Drums rolled, trumpets parped, and an elderly woman with an enormous tuba on her lap (and a pigeon on her head) puffed out her cheeks and blew. Hard.

PAAAAARP!

A rather large spider flew from the tuba. His thick unibrow furrowed with concentration as he whistled through the warm night air, swinging a lasso made from

a strand of shimmering
web above his head.

"Go get them, Colin!"
Mr. Penguin cried.

As he flew,
the spider nodded
in a businesslike
fashion and

took out a notepad from under his bow
tie. He wrote a message on it with a thick
marker pen.

It said I'M ON IT, MR. PENGUIN.

Then he stashed the pad away neatly
before landing with a dramatic roll right
in front of the glamorous lady in the black
dress.

She gasped. And so did everyone else.

The band stopped playing. The dancers all stopped prancing and stared. The only sound was of moths' wings flapping around the lanterns.

The lady narrowed her eyes and scowled. One of her bodyguards lifted his enormous foot to stamp on Colin the spider.

But little did they know that Colin was a kung fu master. And he was more than ready for them.

CHAPTER TWO

FETCH THE BRIEFCASE, MR. PENGUIN!

I n the next few moments, a lot of things happened.

The bodyguard stamped his foot, but Colin was too quick. He sprang up into the air and biffed the gigantic bodyguards on their noses before they knew what was happening—POW! POW! He clonked their heads together, they staggered backward, and the one holding the briefcase dropped it.

The glamorous lady screeched like an angry owl and dived to catch hold of the briefcase. But as she did, Colin swung his web lasso, flung it around her ankle, and yanked her away.

She fell down with a thud. All around her, the crowd started to panic and squeal as she tried furiously to claw back across the floor to her precious briefcase.

From the back of the orchestra, the elderly lady with the pigeon on her head jumped up and yelled, "FETCH THE BRIEFCASE, MR. PENGUIN!"

Mr. Penguin, who'd been gawping at the action with his beak flapping open, leapt to attention.

"Oh yes!" he cried. "Rightio, Edith!"

He hopped down from his conductor's pedestal and began waddling across the dance floor as fast as he could, apologizing very politely to everyone he bumped into.

The band, sensing that something thrilling was about to happen, broke into a raucous, dramatic, and exceedingly parpy piece of music that matched the action perfectly.

The dancers and waiters tottered this way and that in a giddy panic. Tables fell over, champagne glasses shattered on the floor, and chairs were knocked flying as everyone tried to skitter out of the way of whatever was happening. Mr. Penguin ripped off his wig and dinner jacket as he weaved through the confusion of legs,

revealing a little orange satchel slung
across his chest. He grabbed his dashing
Adventurer's hat from the bag and plonked
it sternly on his head. Then he skidded to
a halt, stretched out a flipper, and grabbed
the briefcase. At exactly the same moment,
the glamorous lady broke free from Colin's
web lasso and also snatched at the briefcase.

Time seemed to stand still.

Everyone stopped and stared.

The delicate gold watch on the lady's wrist tick-tocked loudly. Mr. Penguin and the lady glared at each other as they both held the briefcase.

TICK TOCK, TICK TOCK, TICK TOCK...

"GET ON WITH IT, MR. PEN-GUIN," yelled Edith from somewhere in the crowd.

Mr. Penguin slapped the lady's hand with his free flipper. She gasped, and Mr. Penguin didn't hesitate—he wrenched the case away.

"Come on, Colin!" he cried, tucking the briefcase under his flipper and leaping to his feet. "Let's scamper!"

The two friends waddled and weaved their way across the dance floor toward the back exit. Edith and Gordon the pigeon were already waiting there.

"Excellent work, Mr. Penguin!" Edith called, grinning as she and Gordon scampered down the stairs.

Colin and Mr. Penguin were just about to follow her, when THUD—Mr. Penguin skidded and flew face-first into the large belly of one of the bodyguards, which was now blocking the door. With a BOING, Mr. Penguin shot back across the room.

"QUICK, COLIN!" he cried in midair.

"TO THE OTHER EXIT!"

He landed heavily on his bottom, leapt up again, and ran as fast as he could. The two chums swerved toward the other set of doors, but once again they were foiled— the other bodyguard stood in the doorway, snarling and rubbing his fists together.

"Colin," said Mr. Penguin, "we're trapped! There's no escape!" He could feel himself getting quite panicky and a bit hot under his bow tie as the glamorous lady pushed through the crowds toward them.

Luckily, Colin was, as usual, calm as a cucumber. He nudged Mr. Penguin's bottom across the dance floor, toward the edge of the roof.

"Um…Colin…" said Mr. Penguin,

nervously, "there isn't an exit over here! The stairs are thataway!"

He glanced over his shoulder. The lady and her two bodyguards were racing toward them, but Colin had doubled his pace. Soon he and Mr. Penguin were standing right on the edge of the building. Nine stories below them, rickshaws and cars bustled along the busy street. A night market was in full swing, sizzling with rich and exotic smells.

As Mr. Penguin looked down, his head swam and his knobbly knees knocked.

"I hope you're not thinking about jumping off this building!" he hissed out of the side of his beak, glancing sideways at Colin.

His friend was holding up his notepad.

It said HOLD ON.

And then on the next page:

TIGHT.

Mr. Penguin barely had time to read the words before Colin gave him a shove and the two friends hurtled off the edge of the hotel, down to the busy street below.

CHAPTER THREE

A ROARING
ENGINE!

The night air whistled past Mr. Penguin's ears as he fell from the rooftop. In his panic, it was all he could do to hold onto the briefcase with one flipper and clamp his other flipper to his hat.

BUMP!

Mr. Penguin and Colin hit an intricately carved windowsill and bounced like two rubber balls boinging off the walls of a squash court.

"Oh no! Oh no! Oh no!" cried Mr. Penguin. He gritted his beak, waiting to crash on the ground, but suddenly he hit something and pinged right back up into the air. He opened an eyelid a crack and saw that he had bounced off one of the bendy flagpoles at the hotel's main entrance. Mr. Penguin was now flying UPWARD, toward the roof—in the direction of the mean-faced bodyguards and their villainous boss. He didn't know what was worse—hurtling toward the ground, or flying up to meet those brutes with their ham-sized fists.

Luckily, neither of these things happened. In a flash, Colin lassoed his friend with another glistening strand of web and tugged him back down. The pair was once again zooming toward the market below.

Mr. Penguin yelped and closed his eyes.

RRRRRRRIP!

They tore through one of the hotel's canopy shades and—

CRASH! SQUELCH!

—landed in a large crate of satsuma mandarins on the back of a rickshaw.

Breathlessly, Mr. Penguin sat up. Both he and Colin were covered in sticky orange pulp. The briefcase fell open—the lock must have broken in the crash—and Mr. Penguin grabbed the object from inside, shoving it into his satchel. The two Adventurers jumped out of the crate and shook themselves dry(ish).

"Where now?" Mr. Penguin asked, frantically looking about. All around him was a fuzzy blur of activity. Traffic whizzed by, and market stall vendors were shouting about the grub sizzling on their huge pans. Mr. Penguin's tummy grumbled.

Oh! he thought happily, *I could just do with a bite to—*

Colin tapped him on the flipper.

His pad said:

OVER THERE.

And Colin pointed across the street. To Mr. Penguin's surprise, Edith was sitting on the back of an enormous and not-terribly-safe-looking motorbike. Gordon, serene as always, was nestled neatly on top of her headscarf.

Colin grabbed Mr. Penguin by the flipper before he could ask any questions, and they weaved their way across the busy street.

"Yikes!" Mr. Penguin cried as a car whizzed past his beak.

"Crikey!" he yelped as a bike teetering with a tower of parcels narrowly avoided his foot.

"Great prawn crackers!" Mr. Penguin squawked as Colin pushed him out of the way of a racing rickshaw.

Eventually they made it to the other side of the road.

"WHERE DID YOU GET THAT MOTORBIKE FROM, EDITH?" Mr. Penguin shouted over all the noise.

Edith looked a bit sheepish.

"I'VE...UM...BORROWED IT," she yelled, not quite meeting his eye. "BUT DON'T YOU WORRY ABOUT THAT

NOW—JUST HOP ON THE BACK! QUICK, MR. PENGUIN—THEY'RE BEHIND YOU!"

Mr. Penguin looked over his shoulder and squeaked. Sure enough, the two big bruisers from the roof were now in the street, shoving a young man off his motorbike. They hopped onto it and revved the engine, surging through the traffic—right toward Mr. Penguin and his gang of Adventurers.

Edith grabbed Mr. Penguin by the satchel and heaved him onto the motorbike. Colin hopped on behind him, not breaking eye contact with the beefy crooks for a second.

Mr. Penguin wrapped his flippers tightly around Edith's belt bag. With a roar of the engine and a squeal from the tires, they set off in a cloud of dust.

CHAPTER FOUR

IT BELONGS
IN A MUSEUM!

Edith hunched down low over the handlebars and tore through the traffic. The bodyguards followed. Every time Mr. Penguin opened his eyes, they seemed to be getting closer. Behind him, Colin was dancing about like a boxer in the ring, air-punching and waving his pad. It said:

between the two racing motorbikes, with Mr. Penguin's satchel stuck in the middle.

Eventually, one of its seams started to rip.

"COLIN!" Mr. Penguin cried, his heart thumping like a big bass drum. "DO SOMETHING!"

Colin leapt into action. He jumped from the back of the motorbike, onto the bodyguard's shoulder, and biffed him on the nose—KAPOW—before diving back and landing perfectly on Mr. Penguin's shoulder.

The bodyguard let go of the satchel, and Mr. Penguin pulled it close to his chest again.

"HOORAY!" he cheered. "Where to now, Edith?"

Edith furrowed her brow and slithered through the roaring traffic like a snake, but the two beastly bodyguards weren't far behind.

"TO THE AIR BASE!" Edith cried, revving the engine up to full throttle. She slammed her foot on the pedal and skillfully swerved the motorbike down a side street.

She suddenly hunched low again and yelled, "DUCK!"

"Ooh! Where?!" Mr. Penguin asked, looking around brightly. He loved feeding the ducks in the park near his home in Cityville.

"NO!" cried Edith. "DUCK!" And she flattened herself as low as she could go.

Colin pounced on top of Mr. Penguin's head to push it down as Edith drove the motorbike right between the wheels of an enormous garbage truck. The gigantic vehicle roared over their heads.

Behind, the bodyguards tried to follow, but they were far too big.

As Mr. Penguin and his gang of Adventurers escaped into the night, the two brutes crashed headfirst into the truck. They flew off their bike and landed with a disgusting squelch in the back, covered from head to toe in foul-smelling garbage.

A large black car swerved into the side road on two wheels and slammed on the brakes with a dreadful screech, sending a great cloud of dust and exhaust fumes billowing into the air. As the smoke cleared, the glamorous lady from the roof terrace tore off her sunglasses and slapped her beautifully manicured hand against the steering wheel. She was LIVID!

On her chest, the strange brooch glinted in the glow of a nearby streetlight.

My name is Dr. Mesmero, and I am a hypnotist. Actually, I am absolutely and without any doubt the best hypnotist in the world.

I am using this journal to keep track of all the little pieces of my dastardly plan. It also means that, when I have succeeded, I can flip back through this grubby notepad and marvel at just how clever I have been.

The ancient art of hypnotism has been in my family for generations. My father was a hypnotist, and his father and all the fathers before them. However, my skills surprised everyone. I was only a few days old when I managed to hypnotize a nurse in the hospital. Apparently I got the nurse to remove all the other babies from the ward so I didn't have to have to put up with their dreadful crying and stinky diapers.

CHAPTER FIVE

A MIDAIR FISH FINGER SANDWICH

Half an hour later, Mr. Penguin was making himself comfortable in the back of an airplane that Edith had "borrowed."

She'd been quite vague on the details of whom she had borrowed it from and how, but whatever had happened, Edith and Gordon were now in the cockpit, with Mr. Penguin and Colin settled in the back.

Mr. Penguin had to admit that Edith's ability to fly a plane HAD come as a bit of a surprise, just like her being able to ride a motorbike.

"Oh, it's wonderful what you can learn in a library," she'd said when Mr. Penguin asked her. Then she'd bundled him into the back of the plane. There'd been no more time for questions as they'd clattered down the runway and made a sharp climb into the air.

Mr. Penguin looked around the back of the plane. It wasn't sleek like the photographs he'd seen in travel agents' windows in Cityville. In fact, it was a small affair and looked as if it had been cobbled together from any old bits of metal that were going spare. It seemed that it was mainly used for carrying parcels and letters, which was why Mr. Penguin was now wiggling about to get his bottom comfortable amongst some packages.

A deep, rumbling noise was coming from beside him. Colin had plumped himself down in a soft spot, popped his bowler hat over his eyes and fallen asleep. He was now snoring happily. He was obviously having quite an exciting dream, because every few moments he grunted and biffed an imaginary bad guy on the nose with one of his kung fu fighting legs.

KAPOW!

Mr. Penguin wasn't sure what to do with himself. He wasn't the most confident flyer, and the plane did seem to be bobbling about in quite an alarming manner. Really, Mr. Penguin was happiest when he was sitting still and cozy on the ground—in an armchair perhaps—with something delicious in his beak, making its way to his belly. His stomach growled at the thought.

"Of course!" he gasped. "I'll busy myself with a snack!"

As Mr. Penguin reached into his satchel for his emergency fish finger sandwich, he also found the object he'd swiped from under the noses of those fearful brutes in the Golden Pagoda Hotel. As he tucked into the slightly squished sandwich, he turned the object over in his flipper. It seemed like such a lot of fuss over nothing.

It was just a large, heavy stone! The only thing that made it different from any other stone he regularly tripped over in Cityville's In-the-Center-Park was a little line of delicately carved writing wrapped around its middle like a belt.

Mr. Penguin squinted at it, but couldn't make beak nor flipper of what the words said. It certainly wasn't in any language he knew (which wasn't many). *But this stone must be jolly important,* he thought, *with all those people wanting it so badly.*

Mr. Penguin put it carefully back in his bag and finished his sandwich. Then, with his belly full, he nestled down among the parcels and closed his eyes.

He imagined waddling proudly into Cityville University the next morning and handing the stone over to his client, Professor Stout-Girdle. He thought of the

hundreds of dollars she'd promised him as a reward. Just THINK of all the fish finger sandwiches he could buy—even after he'd given Edith, Gordon, and Colin their share.

Mr. Penguin licked his beak happily. Yes…he'd buy lots of fish finger sandwiches. And bow ties…and maybe a jazzy new hat…

And with these happy thoughts, he drifted off to sleep.

* * *

When Mr. Penguin woke up, his flippers were stiff and he had a bit of a numb bottom. He must have been asleep for hours!

Edith was beside him, prodding him urgently in the belly and saying, "Coo-ee! Mr. Penguin!" in hushed tones.

"What…what is it?" Mr. Penguin stammered, blinking groggily. "Are we home? Have we landed in Cityville?"

"Oh no…no…" nattered Edith, "I'd say we have a couple more hours left to go."

"OK…" Mr. Penguin sat up and scratched his hat. "Wait, Edith…if you're here, who's flying the plane?"

"Gordon," said Edith, grinning. "He's ever such a good flyer! But then he should be—he's a pigeon…"

"Right!" said Mr. Penguin. "Um…is everything OK?"

Edith fussed with her belt bag.

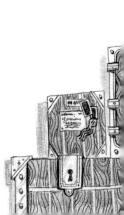

"I think we've got a *little* bit of a problem," she said. "We seem to have made a bit of a booboo. We've run out of gas, and we might be about to crash…"

"CRASH?!" yelped Mr. Penguin, leaping to his feet.

Edith pointed to the window behind Mr. Penguin's head.

"Yes, crash," she said, pointing outside, "into that mountain right there!"

CHAPTER SIX

KNICKERS!

What happened next was a bit of a blur. Mr. Penguin panicked and ran up and down the plane shouting, "WHAT'LL WE DO?! WHAT'LL WE DO?!"

Colin woke up and leapt onto Mr. Penguin's bow tie, bopping him on the beak with a rolled-up woolly vest he'd found in a box somewhere.

That calmed Mr. Penguin right down—but what WERE they going to do? Edith was right; they were about to crash! The engines were spluttering, and the plane was hiccupping through the skies above a treacherously jagged landscape. HUGE mountains were looming ahead out of the dark night sky. There wasn't a moment to lose!

"Are there any parachutes on board?" cried Mr. Penguin.

Colin skittered around the plane looking in all the bags and boxes.

NO, said his pad.

Mr. Penguin's flippers started to quiver and shake, and he racked his brain to think of SOMETHING. No parachutes…

But what about something they could use as a parachute?

"Colin!" said Mr. Penguin, straightening his bow tie. "Where did you find that woolly vest you bopped me with?"

OVER THERE, said Colin's pad. He pointed to a large box labeled:

CONSIGNMENT OF LUXURY UNDERGARMENTS FOR
MME NATTY BLOOMERS'
UNDERWEAR
EMPORIUM
Knickers of Distinction since 1743.
Fifth Avenue, Cityville

PAR AVION

Mr. Penguin took a flying leap, landed in the box, and started flinging the contents over his shoulder.

"WHAT ARE YOU DOING, MR. PENGUIN?" Edith yelled as a pair of tights landed on her head. "WE'RE GOING TO CRASH AT ANY MOMENT!"

Mr. Penguin sat up inside the box and said:

"KNICKERS!"

Edith pursed her lips and tutted. "Really, Mr. Penguin! I know we are about to smash into a mountain, but there's no need to use *that* sort of language—"

"No!" interrupted Mr. Penguin. "Knickers! This box is full of vests and knickers! Really big ones too! Look!"

He held out a giant pair of silky under-pants. They were ENORMOUS! Colin, Mr. Penguin, Edith, and Gordon could have all fitted in one leg and still have had enough room to hold a cocktail party.

"Colin," said Mr. Penguin, "can you spin us some web?"

OF COURSE, said Colin's pad firmly.

"Good! Then I have a plan!"

In no time at all, the Adventurers were standing by the door. Mr. Penguin pushed it open, and the entire cabin filled with rushing, roaring, icy cold air.

The plane shook like a jelly. The left wing clipped the side of one of the mountains, and great plumes of black smoke billowed out into the night. Far below them, snowflakes swirled over rocky hills.

"After three!" shouted Mr. Penguin. His little penguin-y knees were knocking.

"One!"

"Two!"

"Three!"

And they jumped out of the plane.

Four giant pairs of knickers unfolded above their heads, attached to them by fine but strong strands of web.

Mr. Penguin's heart was hammering as the snow-covered mountain rushed to meet them.

He glanced up just in time to see the plane hitting the rocks above them and exploding with a

BANG!

As soon as I could walk I started performing in my father's hypnotic stage shows in little theaters all around the country. The audiences loved me—the tiny child with the extraordinarily powerful gift. When I look back at old photographs, I can see why. I was so adorable with my rosy cheeks, my freckles, my gappy toothed smile, and my tiny stage outfits. I had audiences eating out of my hands—sometimes for real. I often tricked people into believing they were ponies—I fed them sugar lumps on stage whilst the crowd roared with laughter.

Word of my performances spread, and I was soon traveling to faraway lands to put on shows for the rich and famous. I'd hit the big time.

Huge posters of me wearing my trademark dark sunglasses hung outside the biggest theaters in the world. Desperate fans waited outside with their autograph books.

Everywhere I went, my name was in lights.

I was a star!

CHAPTER SEVEN

SOMEONE IS MISSING

Mr. Penguin slowly opened his eyes. Everything was cold and silent and white.

It took him several minutes just lying there on his front to realize that he had landed in a deep snow drift.

His ears were full of ice, and he was knotted up in his giant knickers parachute.

He sat up, untangled himself, and looked about. He was, he discovered, three-quarters of the way up a dark, dangerous, snow-covered mountain. All around him, sharp, jagged peaks jutted up into the inky sky like gigantic shark fins.

Further up the mountain, their plane was lying smashed and smoking. Mr. Penguin shuddered—what if he and his chums had been in it as it crashed into the rocks? The damage to his special Adventurer's hat would have been dreadful…

A voice, wafting through the freezing air, interrupted Mr. Penguin's thoughts.

"COOO-EEEE! Mr. Penguin? Are you OK?"

It was Edith.

Mr. Penguin patted himself down with his flippers just to check. "Yes!" he said. "Are you?"

"Yes, I think so. Although I can't find my belt bag…" There was a brief pause followed by some rustling and a very businesslike bit of cooing.

"Oh! It's OK—Gordon's found it!" Edith cried, delighted. "Well done, Gordon! We'll come and get you, Mr. Penguin! Wait there!"

A couple of minutes later, Mr. Penguin, Edith, and Gordon were huddled and shivering together near the wreckage of the plane. Mr. Penguin was very worried.

"I can't find Colin ANYWHERE," he said. "You don't suppose…" He gulped.

"Now, Mr. Penguin, we won't have any talk like that!" Edith said. "He'll be here somewhere—we just have to find him."

She pushed up the sleeves of her now crumpled and grubby dinner jacket and started searching the tangled mess of metal, packages, and underwear that used to be their plane. Mr. Penguin joined in, wishing he hadn't eaten ALL of his emergency fish finger sandwich already. Mr. Penguin thought there was nothing better in times of Great Worry and Confusion than the feeling of a nice, full tummy.

Edith and Mr. Penguin looked through as much of the plane as they could, all the while calling out for Colin. Gordon helped by standing and blinking on Edith's head.

But all the searching was no good: Colin was nowhere to be found. Mr. Penguin's best friend and No.1 assistant was well and truly lost, and they were stuck up a freezing mountain in the middle of nowhere.

Mr. Penguin sighed deeply and plonked himself heavily on the ground. As soon as he landed, he felt a wiggling from the snow under his bottom. A notepad was thrust into the air.

On it was written:

OUCH!

Mr. Penguin couldn't believe it!

"Colin?" he gasped. "Is that you?"

Scribbling sounds.

Next page: YOU ARE SITTING ON ME.

Then:

HELP!

And finally:

(PLEASE)

Mr. Penguin leapt up, his flippers suddenly a blur of digging action.

Within seconds, Colin popped out of the snow like a cork from a champagne bottle. Mr. Penguin wiped ice from his friend's frozen unibrow.

"HOORAY!" hooted Mr. Penguin. "WE ARE ALL BACK TOGETHER AGAIN!"

He danced about in the snow in a very

giddy fashion. He only stopped when Edith said, "But what's the plan now?"

Well, that burst Mr. Penguin's balloon. What WERE they going to do? They were lost, miles and miles and MILES away from their home in Cityville. (And, Mr. Penguin thought with a tummy grumble, miles away from his favorite sandwiches at the Popular Plaice 24-Hour Diner.)

He looked again at the smoking wreck of the plane and scratched his beak.

"Can you fix it?" he asked Edith.

Edith put her hands on her hips and let out a long, slow whistle.

"Well," she said ponderously, "I could certainly have a go...but

I've left my wrench in one of my parka's pockets back in Cityville."

She rummaged around in her belt bag. "And there's only so much I can do with sticky tape," she said, brandishing a fresh roll.

The four Adventurers stood looking at their plane, each thinking bleak and bewildered thoughts. Then a muffled voice from behind them said "HELLO?" and a small hand tapped Mr. Penguin on the shoulder.

CHAPTER EIGHT

A CLOCKWORK SLEIGH

Mr. Penguin yelped and nearly leapt out of his skin.

"Sssssssh!" hissed the shoulder-tapper. "You'll start an avalanche!"

Mr. Penguin, Colin, Edith, and Gordon whipped around to see who (or what!) was speaking to them. They discovered two small humans, both bundled up in an extraordinary array of knitwear and standing knee-deep in the snow.

"We've come to rescue you!" said the boy human. He pulled his scarf away from his mouth with a glove-covered hand and grinned broadly. "We saw your plane crash into the mountain from our attic!"

The girl human pushed back her bobble hat to reveal a shock of blond hair and two rosy cheeks.

"We were looking through our telescope," she said, "and making notes about the fortress."

(There was no mention of fish finger sandwiches, but Mr. Penguin decided to wait until he knew the children better before bringing up *that* subject.)

As the Adventuring gang followed the children through the snow, Mr. Penguin made sure that the stone was still in his satchel. It was…but it did now have a tiny crack on one side from the crash. Mr. Penguin hoped that Professor Stout-Girdle wouldn't notice it and put the stone safely back in his bag.

"Um…are we walking all the way to the village?" asked Mr. Penguin, who suddenly found himself up to his bow tie in snow. Colin rescued him, as always.

"Of course not," cried the girl. "We're going to go in my clockwork sleigh!"

And suddenly a curious contraption stood before them. It looked like the sort of sleigh Santa Claus rode in, but with no reindeer. Instead, its sides were made up of cogs, wheels, and mechanical moving parts.

The two children helped the Adventurers into the machine and tucked their knees under a snuggly wool blanket.

"My sister made this!" said the boy proudly, as the girl busied herself turning an enormous metal key. "She's a whizz with anything mechanical. In the morning she'll have a look at your plane and see if she can fix it."

Mr. Penguin was just about to say thank-you when the girl turned around in her seat and beamed at them.

"Everyone ready?" she asked gleefully. They all nodded, and with a pull of a lever, the sleigh shuddered and began rising up into the air on great metal, clockwork legs. To Mr. Penguin's disbelief, the sleigh started walking down the mountain through the thick, crunchy snow—as easily as he would waddle around the streets of Cityville!

CHAPTER NINE

SCHNEEDORF-ON-THE-PEAK

Riding on the back of a walking clock work sleigh was an extraordinary experience. Mr. Penguin found it utterly thrilling to be marched down the mountain with snow falling on his head, while toe-wigglingly cozy under a thick blanket.

The twins (Aha! So they WERE twins!) told the Adventurers about their village. Schneedorf-on-the-Peak was one of the highest villages in the world—perched on the side of a dizzyingly tall mountain. There was another mountain across the valley that was taller, but no one lived there. The twins swapped odd looks when the boy said that and quickly changed the subject to the weather. It ALWAYS snowed in Schneedorf, they said.

Mr. Penguin wasn't sure how he felt about that. He liked the *idea* of snow, but preferred to see it from somewhere warm, through closed windows, and with a hot fish finger sandwich in his flippers. Being cold reminded him of a time before he was an

Adventurer, when he'd lived in The Frozen South, with endless miles of empty, freezing, gleaming white coldness. He shuddered at the thought.

The village was a lovely higgledy-piggledy collection of buildings under pretty snow-covered roofs. Wiggly plumes of smoke snaked peacefully from chimneys and jolly-colored decorations were strung above the steep, narrow streets. It was so quiet and calm compared to busy Cityville.

The sleigh slowed down in a small town square that sloped at quite a hair-raising angle. Tall, rickety-looking shops and houses stood on three sides, with the most enormous ornate clock the Adventurers had ever seen on the fourth side. Even Colin was impressed.

WOW, said his pad. And Mr. Penguin agreed wholeheartedly.

"That's the King Ludvig von Clonker Memorial Clock," the boy said. "It was built hundreds of years ago to commemorate King Ludvig's skiing skills. He used to come here every winter, and one time he managed a *very* complicated trick involving several star jumps, a couple of somersaults, and a dance with a feather-edged fan, all in midair!"

"Did he really?" asked Mr. Penguin, amazed.

"Oh yes!" said the boy. "And he only broke six bones doing it."

"We are famous for three things," said his sister. "How high our village is, our giant clock, and the International Rodent Ga…" She trailed off, glancing at her brother, who was suddenly looking very glum.

Mr. Penguin didn't notice—he was too busy ogling the clock—but Colin jotted down HMMM on his notepad.

"I look after the clock," the girl said. "Before me, it was our granddad. But it's a bit broken at the moment. The clockwork cuckoo keeps flying out bottom first, and one of its mechanical eyes won't stop twitching."

"But you'll get it fixed, won't you?" asked her brother.

His sister nodded as she pulled the large lever, and the sleigh came to a stop. They were outside a bakery café with warm yellow light spilling from the windows. A pink and white sign above the door proclaimed:

Frau Strudel's Haus of Strudel

"And this…" announced the girl, "…is home!" The smell of hot food wafting out of the door made Mr. Penguin's stomach growl.

While the sleigh lowered itself, Colin tapped Mr. Penguin on the flipper with one of his spidery legs.

He held up his notepad:

I THINK THESE CHILDREN ARE HIDING SOMETHING.

"What do you mean?" hissed Mr. Penguin. "They just have loads of layers on."

Colin rolled his eyes and scribbled on his pad again.

But there was no time to ask Colin what he meant. The two children hopped from their seats to help the Adventurers out. Colin stashed his pad back under his bowler hat.

"With all this excitement," said the boy, "we haven't introduced ourselves! I'm Dieter, and—"

"I'm Lisle!" said his twin, as Mr. Penguin tumbled headfirst into a snow drift. She pulled him out and he thanked her, dusting snow off his bow tie.

"That's Edith Hedge," Mr. Penguin said. "On her head is Gordon, and this is Colin." Mr. Penguin pulled himself up to his full (not very tall) height, puffed out his chest and added, "And I am Mr. Penguin, Adventurer. And Penguin."

Dieter gasped, his rosy cheeks draining of color until they were white as snow. He staggered backward against the bakery window.

"Y-y-y-you're Mr. Penguin?" Dieter stammered. "THE Mr. Penguin? From Cityville?"

Mr. Penguin nodded, feeling less confident now that *was* actually who he was. Dieter looked at Mr. Penguin with wide, goggly eyes, then gulped and ran off into the night.

To begin with, being famous was exciting. Everyone made an enormous fuss of me wherever I went. Anything I wanted, I could have. Ice cream at midnight. Jelly for breakfast. A new pet hamster in a gilded cage topped with a large satin bow.

The money came rolling in, but I soon got tired of it all. The constant shows and the traveling left very little room for anything else. I didn't go to school, but I taught myself from books. My favorite subjects were science and engineering.

Then I met a world-famous scientist on a ship while I was traveling to the Distant East. I snuck into one of his lectures on a boring, rainy afternoon and was surprised to find it thrilling.

As soon as we docked, I went straight to the nearest bookstore and bought all his books. After that, I wanted nothing more than to be alone to read them and to lose myself in experiments and inventing things.

But every time I took out my books, I had to put them away again to get into costume, have my face smeared with sticky makeup, and be pushed out into the spotlight. It made me very unhappy and very, very angry.

CHAPTER TEN

A LITTLE LIGHT SNOOPING

Nobody knew what to make of Dieter's sudden disappearance. Colin flipped back through his pad until he found the ? note from earlier and held it up.

"Well…" muttered Mr. Penguin. "Quite odd, yes."

Then the door to the bakery flew open, and a very tall woman with rosy cheeks stood there beaming. She was wearing a neat blouse with a piecrust collar and a frilly apron covered with jam splodges.

"Hallo! I'm Helga Strudel, Dieter and Lisle's mother. Welcome to my bakery. Now come in, you must be as chilly as snowmen!"

Everyone shuffled into the warm and allowed this friendly new person to fuss over them—even Colin!

"Where's Dieter?" said Helga.

Lisle's cheeks turned pink.

"Oh," she said, "I think he's just… er…gone to get something. I'll go and find him!"

Helga nodded at her daughter and turned to the Adventurers.

"Now I want you to go to the twins' room in the attic and make yourself at home. There are plenty of sweaters there for you to get cozy in. Then come back down here. I'll have some fresh hot cocoa ready and something nice and warm to tuck into. You must be famished!"

As if on cue, Mr. Penguin's tummy grumbled loudly. He quickly leapt onto the stairs, saying, "That sounds

GGGGGRRRRRRRREAT!" which just about hid the noise.

Mr. Penguin and his gang of Adventurers trooped off up to the attic. The bakery was a very tall, slim building that wiggled and jiggled this way and that up rickety old staircases. Mr. Penguin decided that if he had to be away from his own cozy home in Cityville, then this funny, wonky cake shop was the best place to be.

Thick, jazzy-patterned sweaters were scattered on one of the twins' beds. Within a few minutes, Edith and Mr. Penguin were warmly wrapped in their new knitwear. Gordon was feeling very pleased with himself in his nice new bobble hat.

There wasn't a sweater small enough for Colin, but he didn't mind. The cold air wafting through his bushy unibrow kept his senses sharpened, and he didn't want any knitwear to tangle him up should he have to leap into kung fu action. There was definitely something odd going on here. He said so to Mr. Penguin.

"Hmmm," said Mr. Penguin, as he turned around in front of a mirror and admired his snazzy sweater. "I think we're all feeling a bit wobbly from our crash landing. But let's have a look around just in case…"

Mr. Penguin put his flippers on his hips. He knew it was a bit naughty to rummage around someone's room without asking, but he couldn't resist a bit of light snooping.

One wall of the bedroom was covered in pictures of engines and motors. Beneath it, tools spilled out from under the bed.

"Must be Lisle's side…" mused Mr. Penguin, scratching his beak thoughtfully.

Dieter's side was much more organized. The bed was neatly made, with a tall tower of books, all about hamster training, stacked in order of size on the bedside table. On the wall, pinned up in rows, were photographs of a hamster and of Dieter beaming beside the hamster. Brightly colored rosettes were dotted between them.

"Oh!" said Mr. Penguin. "Dieter must have a nice pet hamster!"

"Yes," said Edith. "That must be its cage over there… but the cage is empty."

Mr. Penguin waddled over to investigate. The cage had all sorts of tubes and tunnels and viewing platforms. There was even a little hamster-sized sauna on the top level! But there was no hamster. Mr. Penguin whipped out his gigantic magnifying glass and looked very closely at it all.

"How odd," he said. "I wonder where it's gone?"

His eyes fell onto a pile of papers beside the cage. Every sheet was full of carefully handwritten notes. Mr. Penguin and Edith couldn't help but peek at them. (Edith had to hold them at arm's length as the writing was tiny and she'd brought the wrong specs.)

Thursday
9:54 PM
Lights observed in the fortress and
smoke from the chimneys.

Friday
3:26 AM
Woken by strange whispery hissing
sounds—seem to come from the walls.

Friday
7:22 AM
Colonel Tuftybum has vanished! He's
the 127th one!

Friday
8:00 AM
I really miss Colonel Tuftybum.

Friday
11:57 PM
More smoke and lights from fortress.
Still no sign of Colonel Tuftybum.

Mr. Penguin straightened up. "Who is Colonel Tuftybum? And what fortress?"

Just then, an eraser whistled through the air and clonked him on the head. "OUCH!" he cried. He looked to see where it had come from and saw Colin waving as he dangled from a telescope poking out of the attic window.

Colin held up his pad:

LOOK THROUGH HERE.

Mr. Penguin did as Colin said. He gasped. Through the telescope he could clearly see a very grim-looking building clinging to the top of the tallest and most pointy mountain, surrounded by sharp rocky peaks.

"That must be the fortress!" he said, and a shiver ran down from his hat to his bottom and right into his shoes. "What on earth is going on?"

Suddenly, a great hullabaloo of voices came from downstairs. Edith adjusted her belt bag decisively. "I think we should go down and find out."

Mr. Penguin gulped. He had a creeping, neck-shivering feeling that whatever it was, it was going to be very dangerous indeed.

I soon got terribly bored of my hypnotism act. Night after night, I hypnotized the audience to believe they were chickens so they'd squawk and strut around on stage to make their rich friends laugh.

After each show, I felt cross that I was using my hypnotic talent in such a silly fashion. There had to be better things I could do with it...

Shortly after my ninth birthday, my diabolical plan began to form. I'd spent the day in bed reading a particularly thrilling and complicated book about radio waves. I was interrupted by a knock at my hotel room door—it was my parents. They were dressed and ready for my performance that evening, and they both looked livid.

"What are you doing still in your pajamas?" cried my mother. "You ought to be in costume and ready for tonight's show!"

I protested, pretended to have a headache, and refused to move.

"There are thousands of very important people coming to see you!" said my father. "You HAVE to perform!"

Before I knew what was happening, my book had been snatched from my hand and thrown into the hotel room fire, and I was being wrestled into my costume and pushed on stage.

Anger bubbled away inside me like a boiling kettle as I stood under the hot stage lights. I felt different. Changed.

I decided to try something new that night. I wanted to see how many people I could hypnotize at once. I already knew my power worked on small groups, as I often got members of the audience up on stage to conga around—quite a sight when it involved members of the Royal Family. But could I hypnotize more?

I took off my trademark dark glasses to find out...

CHAPTER ELEVEN

A PARTY
(OF SORTS)

The bakery downstairs was now full of chattering people. Dieter and Lisle took Mr. Penguin by the flippers and pulled him, Colin, Edith, and Gordon through the gaggle of people. They arrived at a table in the window loaded with mugs of hot cocoa and platefuls of treats.

"Oh!" said Mr. Penguin cheerfully. "Are we having a party?"

He crossed his flippers behind his back, hoping that some nice fish paste sandwiches had been rustled up for him. (Mr. Penguin knew fish fingers would be hard to find up a mountain.)

But Mr. Penguin's cheerfulness vanished when he saw the crowd's faces. Instead of being jolly, everyone looked very serious and worried.

"Whatever's the matter?" gasped Edith. "What's happened?"

Dieter began talking away at full speed.

"I knew you'd come, Mr. Penguin!" he said. "Lisle thought you'd be too busy, but I said that even if you *were* you'd still whizz over here to solve this mystery! So I posted my letter to you and waited and waited and then I couldn't believe it… THE Mr. Penguin just landed—well, crashed, really—on our mountain. I've gathered everyone together so you can start right away!"

Dieter stood grinning with flushed cheeks and huge, excited eyes.

Mr. Penguin had been shoveling strudel into his mouth and had crumbs on his bow tie and jammy splodges all over his beak. But

MISSING! HAVE YOU SEEN THIS HAMSTER?

now he stopped with his fork in midair.

"I'm sorry," he said, "but I'm very confused. What letter? What's happening? What am I helping with?"

"My letter—about Colonel Tuftybum?" cried Dieter.

I BEG YOUR PARDON? said Colin's pad. His eyes were boggling under his unibrow. COLONEL BUM?

"Tuftybum," corrected Lisle. "Colonel Tuftybum is Dieter's hamster. He's got a very tufty sort of bottom." She turned to her brother. "I think you need to explain right from the beginning."

Dieter took a deep breath and began. Mr. Penguin, Colin, Edith, and Gordon listened carefully, their mouths flapping wider and wider as his story continued.

Everyone now rammed in the café had come to Schneedorf for the 32nd International Rodent Games. Their pampered pets would be spending two weeks competing in shows and games in the hope of winning gold medals and special prizes. It was a huge event, but unfortunately none of it had gone ahead.

The night before the competition should have begun, rodents started to disappear. They just vanished in the middle of the night, leaving their cages empty and their exercise wheels motionless. Each morning the rodent owners woke to find more creatures gone. Instead of watching the competition, the villagers and visitors had spent every day searching for their pets.

"But it was no good. We can't find them anywhere," said Dieter sadly.

What in the name of trout burgers could have happened to them? wondered Mr. Penguin. *Who would want to steal a hamster or a mouse?* It seemed so unlikely. Then another thought sent a shiver down his flippers: *What if the hamster thief decides to steal penguins too?*

Lisle interrupted his thoughts. "And there've been other strange things happening, haven't there, Dieter?"

Dieter nodded. His face was pale and anxious, like everyone's in the room.

Lisle explained that for several weeks there had been odd noises coming from the abandoned fortress across the valley— on the mountain known as Old Grandfather Grimm.

"At first," said Lisle, "I thought I was imagining it all. I woke up in the middle of the night and saw lights in the windows, but I just thought my eyes were a bit sleepy and playing tricks on me. But then the next evening, Dieter saw it too!"

Over the next few days, more lights had appeared—and then plumes of smoke, too. When the wind blew a certain way, they could hear banging and drilling noises, with the odd hiss and whirr.

"But the thing is," said Helga, dusting flour off her apron, "that fortress has been abandoned for as long as I can remember..."

"And there's no way to get to it," an elderly woman piped up at the back of the room. She was so wrapped up in knitwear she looked like a sheep. "Old Grandfather Grimm is treacherous—all jagged points and falling boulders. You'd have to be bonkers to even *try* to climb it!"

"So you see," said Dieter, "something very sinister and strange is going on here. And that's why I wrote to you, and that's why you came, isn't it, Mr. Penguin?"

Mr. Penguin looked around the room. Dozens of eyes blinked back at him hopefully. He gulped and wiped jam off his beak with a napkin.

"The thing is…" said Mr. Penguin, "I haven't received any mail, because we've all been away on a case. We just crashed here by accident."

Heavy sighs flew around the bakery.

"And..." continued Mr. Penguin quietly, "we really do need to get back to Cityville. We've got an important delivery to make." He thought of the carved stone hidden in his satchel upstairs.

"Well, you won't get to Cityville any time soon!" an old man in a bobble hat said from the back of the room. "The main road up to our village is blocked. There was a miniavalanche the other night, and the road is full of snow and rocks and boulders! People from the village in the valley are digging their way through, but it's going to take days..."

Mr. Penguin bit his beak anxiously. This wasn't good news. They couldn't deliver the rescued stone to Professor Stout-Girdle if they were stranded up a mountain.

"But now you're here, you'll help us, won't you?" asked Dieter.

Mr. Penguin looked around the room. How would he ever find all these missing pets? And he was willing to bet his last fish finger sandwich that whatever was going on at the fortress would be terribly, knee-knockingly dangerous.

He glanced at Edith and Gordon to see what they thought. Edith adjusted her belt bag, her mouth a line of determination. Gordon just blinked—but he never said much anyway. Mr. Penguin looked down at Colin.

IT IS A THUMBS-UP FROM ME, said the pad.

OR IT WOULD BE IF I HAD THUMBS.

Mr. Penguin gulped again and then nodded.

"We'll do it," he said nervously. "We'll take on the case!"

Everyone in the bakery cheered, and for the first time that evening it did feel a bit like a party!

"Let's start right away!" cried Lisle. "Dieter and I have been investigating, and we've got lots of things to show you!"

The villagers finished their hot cocoa and shuffled out of the bakery, chatting excitedly. They were still looking anxious, but they seemed a lot more hopeful about finding their precious pets.

Dieter and Lisle helped their mum clear the tables while Mr. Penguin finished his third slice of strudel—he needed it to steady his nerves. Gordon had swallowed a cinnamon bun whole, and Edith walloped him on the back until it flew out across the room. Then he tried to eat it again.

So it was only Colin who noticed a man dressed all in black and wearing round sunglasses (odd because it was dark outside) stand up from a shadowy corner and leave the bakery. A flash of light caught a small badge on his lapel, which looked like it might have been an eye in a circle.

A chill bristled through Colin's unibrow as he watched the man slip out of the building. Colin took out his pad and wrote HMMMMMM...

The smaller than usual letters meant he was whispering. The underlining meant he was VERY suspicious.

ACTION STATIONS!

Back up in their attic bedroom, Dieter and Lisle spread out their clues on the floor. Mr. Penguin looked at it all VERY closely through his magnifying glass.

There was so much stuff—notes about strange activity in the fortress, names of all the missing pets with the dates and times when they vanished, and even an old book from the library that contained some interesting information about the fortress itself.

Mr. Penguin read it out loud in his nice reading-out-loud voice.

The fortress on Old Grandfather Grimm was built over two centuries ago. It remains the highest castle in the world and has an intriguing history.

It was designed and built for Herr Friedrich Grimm (after whom the mountain is named). He wanted to move from his home in the nearby village of Schneedorf-on-the-Peak to somewhere more remote. He was a very rich and eccentric man who didn't like people and would hide in the pantry when visitors knocked on the door. He wanted to live somewhere quiet where he could be alone with his pets, and on top of one of the tallest mountains in the world seemed an ideal location.

Not much is known about the fortress, but it is believed to be a warren of rooms with many trapdoors, hidden doorways, and secret entrances.

There used to be a path up to the fortress from the valley below to enable food and supplies to be delivered, but over the years the path has become so overgrown it is now just a tangle of thick, thorny branches guarded by ferocious wild bears and wolves. It is very dangerous and any attempts to climb the mountain would be foolish— unless you want to end up as bear food.

After Herr Grimm died, the fortress began crumbling away and has been abandoned for centuries.

BUT SOMEONE *IS* LIVING UP THERE, said Colin's pad.

Edith sniffed. "Well, I don't know why they'd bother. Looks ever so gloomy, and not a single net curtain in the place…"

"But how did they get up there?" said Dieter. "It's even MORE dangerous now.

All the old paths and bridges have been destroyed by avalanches or are covered in thick ice and snow."

"Are we sure that the missing pets and the fortress are linked?" Mr. Penguin asked. "Maybe these are two separate cases?"

Colin looked at Mr. Penguin with his mouth open. He wasn't used to his friend asking such sensible questions.

"We wondered about that too…" said Dieter. "But both things happened at the same time—the noises and lights at the fortress, and our pets disappearing. They MUST be connected."

"What are we going to do?" asked Lisle.

All eyes swiveled to Mr. Penguin once again. Well, most of the eyes. One of Gordon's was roving around, seemingly lost, but that was nothing unusual.

Oh dear, thought Mr. Penguin, *what ARE we going to do?* He put his flippers behind his back and started to pace about the room. He hoped this suggested he was thinking Cunning and Clever Thoughts. In fact, his mind was as jumbled as a big plate of spaghetti.

"Ooh!" thought Mr. Penguin. "A plate of spaghetti!" That would be nice right now. Then he made himself focus on the problem at hand.

What would Butch Peril, the brave Adventurer from Mr. Penguin's favorite books, do? Mr. Penguin tapped the side of his head and tried to remember something—anything! Then inspiration struck! A trick Butch used in the book *CAPTURED: Red-handed! The Paint Factory Mystery!*

"Well," said Mr. Penguin, "we must try to catch the thief red-handed, just as they are trying to steal another rodent."

Everyone thought that was a marvelous idea. Indeed, Colin's mouth flapped open so widely that he had to close it with one of his feet.

Mr. Penguin outlined his plan, which mainly involved dressing someone up as a hamster and putting them in the cage and then everyone taking it in turns to keep watch. The pet thief would hopefully try to steal the "hamster," and the lookout would jump out of their hiding place and shout "AHA!" very loudly and catch the burglar in the act.

"But who are we going to dress up as the hamster?" asked Edith. "I'm not sure I'll fit in that little cage, not if I want to keep my belt bag with me."

Everyone looked at Mr. Penguin again.

"Oh yes," he said, "it would be better if it was someone small." He slowly turned to Colin and smiled his best winning smile.

Colin scribbled frantically.

ABSOLUTELY NOT, said Colin's pad.

I AM NOT DRESSING UP AS A HAMSTER.

More frantic scribblings.

I SHOULD KEEP WATCH SO I CAN DO MY KUNG FU IF THINGS BECOME DANGEROUS.

He underlined "DANGEROUS" three times, so Mr. Penguin knew not to push any further.

"Who else can do it then?" said Lisle.

A tapping sound made everyone turn around. It was Gordon pecking at his own reflection in the mirror. Mr. Penguin grinned a beaky grin.

I started my performance as usual by picking a couple of people to come up on stage. I quickly hypnotized them into believing they'd just sat down on a hedgehog, and they were soon hopping about the stage trying to remove prickles from their bottoms whilst the audience roared with laughter.

Then I hypnotized a few more people to be under my spell. Then five more. Then ten. My eyes were fizzing with electricity by the time I had fifty people under my control.

I looked out into the audience, daring myself to control more. A sea of people watched me, their tiny opera glasses glinting in the theater lights. Was it possible to hypnotize the whole room?

I focused my mind. I concentrated my powers into my eyeballs. I aimed my gaze at the audience. Everything fizzed and rippled. The effect was immediate.

Silence.

Nobody moved.

Everyone was looking at me with blank faces, waiting for my command. I felt so powerful! It sizzled all over me and made my hair stand up on end.

What could I make this huge room of people do?

Or rather, I thought wickedly, what COULDN'T I make them do?

CHAPTER THIRTEEN

MASTER OF DISGUISE

It was almost midnight, and the trap was set.

Gordon was happily standing in the sawdust in Colonel Tuftybum's cage, dressed in his new hamster costume (quickly made from cotton wool and sticky tape).

Mr. Penguin was hiding behind a curtain, keeping watch. Everyone else was asleep. Colin had taken the previous shift and was now lying upside down in the bin on a bed of crumpled paper and a banana skin. He was still *meant* to be on high alert, but he was actually snoring like a motorbike engine while doing the odd, sleepy kung fu kick.

KA-yawn-POW!

It had been a busy night putting Mr. Penguin's plan into action. While Edith and Colin squeezed Gordon into his costume and popped him in the cage, Mr. Penguin and the twins had taken a snow-crunching walk around the town square. They'd talked in loud, clear voices about the new hamster in Lisle and Dieter's bedroom above the bakery. They wanted any thief who was ear-waggling to know *exactly* where to burgle next.

Then Mr. Penguin had done lots of pre-tend yawning and shouted about how tired everyone was and that they would all abso-lutely *definitely* fall asleep immediately.

Then they'd all bustled back to the bakery to wait.

Behind the curtain, Mr. Penguin didn't need to pretend to yawn—he was doing it for real. The last twenty-four hours had been bonkers, and his eyelids were drooping.

He slapped his face with a flipper. "COME ON, MR. PENGUIN!" he scolded himself in a whisper. "This all depends on you. You need to catch this thief—then you'll be able to have a good sleep and after that a lovely breakfast!"

Breakfast! Now, *that* was a jolly thought!

Mr. Penguin closed his eyes and thought happily about warm pastries and nice cups of tea. Maybe even some fish paste on hot toast… And with that, Mr. Penguin started to snore.

The von Clonker clock struck midnight, and all was still.

In a storm drain opposite the bakery, two glowing yellow eyes blinked. The owner of the eyes glanced about. When it was sure it was alone, it slithered out from its hiding place and wriggled across the snowy cobbles. It shimmied silently up the bakery's drainpipe, onto the roof, and glided across the tiles. Then it carefully ducked its head into the attic through the gap in the window left open for the telescope to poke through.

Everyone was asleep—two children in their beds, a large hairy spider in the bin, an elderly woman with a belt bag on a cot, and a small, rather portly penguin poorly hidden behind a curtain. He was snoring, but kept licking his beak and mumbling about fish finger sandwiches.

And there, in a very fancy cage, was the reason for the creature's visit: a hamster, standing in the sawdust, cooing. The intruder slithered over, but paused as it got closer.

Hmmm…

The animal in the cage looked like a rather unusual sort of hamster. Most *unusual* indeed. But the Boss had been clear: steal every rodent in the village.

The creature opened the door with its tail and carefully picked up the hamster in its mouth. Then it slithered back to the window. But it was just a little bit too hasty. As it wriggled outside, it knocked the telescope, which clattered to the floor. The window slammed shut and trapped the end of the creature's tail. The creature panicked, trying to pull itself free. The strange hamster in its mouth started to coo in a bewildered manner.

Mr. Penguin's eyes snapped open. What was that noise? What was happening? Was it time for breakfast?

He glanced about. Was someone in the room? The cage on the desk was empty! Where was Gordon?

Then he took a flying leap toward the window with his unibrow furrowed and his kung fu legs kicking.

KAPOW!

Mr. Penguin, however, was *not* in control of the situation. Instead, he was swirling about like a tornado, with his satchel flipping about, swiping everything off every surface. BANG! CRASH!

As Colin jumped toward the window, Mr. Penguin collided with him and Colin went boinging back across the room. He hit the door and slid to the floor with his head spinning.

The snake managed to free itself with a heave, and the window slammed shut.

"GORDON! HE'S TAKEN GORDON!" cried Edith. "SOMEBODY DO SOMETHING!"

She dashed across the room and threw the window wide open. Icy air blasted into the room as Edith watched the snake with Gordon (unflustered) in its mouth rattle down the roof tiles and over the gutter.

Colin shook his head to clear the swirl of stars and little Mr. Penguin images that were dancing around him, then took a flying leap. He bounced off Mr. Penguin's tummy again—BOING!—and shot right out of the open window.

"Quick!" yelled Dieter and Lisle. Without wasting a moment, they ran out of the room and down the stairs with Edith at their heels. Mr. Penguin waddled as fast as he could behind them.

They burst out of the front door onto the snowy street just in time to see the snake, Gordon, and then Colin slide down the side of the bakery and over the snow-covered canopy above the shop windows. A mini-avalanche fell in a big lump on the Adventurers and landed in a pile on the pavement.

The snake dithered—snow had blocked its storm drain. How was it going to escape?

The Adventurers grabbed at it all at once, bumping their heads together and falling on their bottoms in the snow. In the confusion, the snake made a wiggly dash for it across the town square, the creature glowing in the light of the enormous clock.

KAPOW! Colin kung fu kicked his way out of his snowy prison and gave chase, skittering and sliding across the icy ground while holding up his pad. It said:

STOP!

and

WAIT!

and also

I WILL CATCH YOU!

Mr. Penguin, Edith, and the twins followed Colin, pleading for the snake to drop Gordon.

How do *I get myself into these situations?* thought Mr. Penguin, puffing and panting his way across the town square. He had to run with both flippers holding his hat firmly in place.

Sleepy faces, woken by the commotion, appeared at windows. Soon a yawning crowd had staggered out into the streets in their pajamas, many with rollers still in their hair.

The snake slithered between all the legs and glanced over what would be its shoulder (if it had a shoulder). The spider and the penguin were gaining on it! The snake doubled its speed. It was exhausting—the funny-looking hamster in its mouth was really rather heavy!

Eventually, the snake found another storm drain. Mr. Penguin and Colin took a giant leap to catch it, but it was too quick

and slithered into the hole. Colin went to follow it, but Mr. Penguin grabbed him.

BUT IT'S GETTING AWAY, said Colin's pad.

Mr. Penguin tried to answer, but was completely out of puff.

"You can't…follow it…Colin," he managed after a full minute of wheezing. "There could…be more snakes…waiting to…gobble you up!" Then he threw himself on the ground and wafted his pink face with his hat.

By now, Edith and the twins had arrived beside them. Edith turned around and faced the villagers. "Where does that drain go?" she demanded. "We'll have to follow it to get my Gordon back!"

A very elderly, wrinkly old man stepped forward. He looked like a tortoise in a nightshirt. "My old granddad told me our drains connected to ones that came from...from the fortress..."

Everyone looked at the fortress. It rose grimly above a thick, freezing mist, with dim yellow lights in the thin windows and smoke billowing out of its chimneys.

"Come on!" said Edith, tightening the strap of her belt bag. "Let's go!"

"But you'll never climb it!" said the old man. "There are bears and wolves and ice and thorns!"

Edith stood silently, chewing her bottom lip and looking at Mr. Penguin. He shifted, feeling discombobulated. The other mountain sounded *very* dangerous, and that snake had big teeth that Mr. Penguin was sure would love to nibble on a penguin. But on the other hand, Gordon was their friend. More than that—he was one of their special Adventuring gang!

Mr. Penguin took a deep breath, stood up, and plonked his hat back on his head.

"We *must* rescue Gordon!" he said, fussing with his bow tie. "And all the other pets that are trapped in the fortress!"

Then he said, "But I'm not quite sure how we'll get there…"

The crowd cheered—just as the von Clonker clock struck half past midnight. A heavy BONG sounded, a door flew open, and out popped a large metal bird, bottom first. It had one eyelid twitching and only one of its wings flapping. The mechanical bird turned, opened its beak, and hollered an awful tinny verse of the national anthem, then disappeared inside the clock.

"That really needs fixing," tutted someone in the crowd.

Beside Mr. Penguin, Lisle was staring at the clock. Her eyes gleamed.

"We are going to *fly* to the fortress!" she announced.

Everyone HURRAH-ed again—including Mr. Penguin. Then he stopped and said, "Hang on—our plane's in tatters!"

Lisle grinned. "I think there's another way…"

As I hypnotized every single person in the audience that night, you could have heard a pin drop. All eyes were on me, and the air tingled and fizzed and rippled and wobbled.

It was incredible! I felt I could have done anything! But then my father had to ruin it. He'd heard the silence from my dressing room backstage, where he'd been combing his mustache. He ran in to see what was happening and quickly realized what I had managed to do. He darted onto the stage and slipped my dark glasses over my eyes, breaking the spell.

Polite applause broke out even though no one in the theater knew what had just happened. When I looked at my father, I could tell he was angry, but also frightened. I was too powerful. He told me later that I had looked like a wild animal on the stage.

Shortly after that, I packed my bags and ran away.

And I have been working on my Diabolical Plan ever since.

CHAPTER FIFTEEN

THE STRANGER IN BLACK

L isle's plan was, Mr. Penguin thought, both completely brilliant and utterly bonkers.

She was going to turn the mechanical cuckoo from the von Clonker clock into a clockwork plane so they could use it to fly over to the fortress.

Mr. Penguin thought it sounded like a mad idea, but then his stomach growled. "Maybe it'll sound more sensible once we've had some breakfast," he suggested.

"Breakfast?!" said Edith. "Mr. Penguin, we must start straight away!"

Mr. Penguin groaned. Gordon being kidnapped had made him feel all worried and crinkly inside, and when that happened his tummy started rumbling.

They all headed over to the clock.

As they walked, Colin squinted at the sleepy villagers ambling back to their beds. He was trying to spot that strange man in the dark glasses he'd seen in the bakery.

He couldn't help feeling that the man was somehow involved in all this funny business. But as hard as he looked, he couldn't see the stranger anywhere, and that made him even more suspicious.

Lisle unlocked a small door at the base of the clock tower and ushered everyone inside.

Mr. Penguin stared around, flabbergasted. Thousands of tiny cogs turned and whirred and clicked, and the huge iron hands of the clock high above them ticktocked in a very stately fashion.

Lisle grabbed her toolbox and got cracking, with Edith helping (it turned out she was an expert with a blowtorch). Dieter fetched and carried anything his sister wanted, and Colin was there to provide any brute strength they needed. Mr. Penguin decided that he was best suited to supervising proceedings, and he did this by poking his beak into everything and touching things that he shouldn't.

Colin, sensing an accident was just waiting to happen, led Mr. Penguin to the side and told him on his notepad all about the mysterious stranger in black. He even drew a picture of him.

"Hmmm," said Mr. Penguin, "that IS very suspicious. I wonder who he is and why he's here? He doesn't sound like the sort to be a hamster owner... I think we should see if we can find him." His stomach grumbled and he added casually, "We could start at the bakery, perhaps?"

It turned out the mysterious stranger wasn't in the café at all (but the two chums looked under all the tables AND under some of the larger cakes on display in the window, just to be sure).

However, while they were there, Mr. Penguin and Colin took the opportunity to fill their bellies up with delicious pastries and tea.

Then, after they had delivered a basket full of food and a large flask of hot cocoa to Dieter, Lisle, and Edith, Mr. Penguin whipped his magnifying glass out again and he and Colin began to search Schneedorf-on-the-Peak for the man in black.

Mr. Penguin wasn't really sure how his magnifying glass was going to help, but he thought it showed the villagers that he was very much on top of things (even though he really wasn't).

The two friends snooped around the village.

They looked around dark corners.

They listened at doors and windows.

They shifted great piles of snow, looking for hidden hidey-holes.

Well, Colin shifted piles of snow. Mr. Penguin supervised

while polishing his magnifying glass on his sweater. It had become very dirty from being kept in his satchel with that grubby old stone.

After several long hours of looking, Mr. Penguin huffed and said, "Colin, this strange man of yours seems to have disappeared off the side of the mountain! Have you been a silly sausage and imagined him?"

With just the slightest movement of his unibrow, Colin gave Mr. Penguin a look which said that Mr. Penguin had proved *himself* to be the silliest sausage by asking that question. Colin NEVER imagined things.

Unsuccessful in their search, they mooched back to the clock to see how Lisle, Dieter, and Edith were doing.

The workshop inside the clock was now an absolute disaster. The floor was littered with cogs and tools and great splashes of stinky oil. But in the middle of the mess, glinting in the light that streamed in dramatically through the glass panels of the clock face at just the right angle, was the most incredible machine.

Mr. Penguin couldn't believe his eyes.

CHAPTER SIXTEEN

A MARVELOUS, MECHANICAL FLYING MACHINE

W ow!" gasped Mr Penguin.

Edith gave the cuckoo plane a final polish with a clean hanky from her belt bag.

The clockwork bird looked sleek and shiny and ready for action, with a small propeller in its beak. Its wonky eyelid was no longer twitching, and there was space for a pilot and passengers in the back.

"Lisle!" cried Mr. Penguin. "This is BRILLIANT!"

Colin was grinning all the way up to his unibrow and scampered underneath it to check out the well-polished cogs and mechanisms.

His notepad slid out from under the aircraft. It asked:

HOW DOES IT WORK?

"Easy!" Lisle wiped her greasy hands on the front of her now filthy trousers.

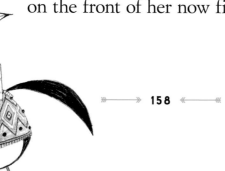

(Dieter, Mr. Penguin noticed, was watching in horror. He was still as neat as a pin, without even a splodge of oil on his pajamas.) Lisle slotted an enormous metal key into a lock rather unfortunately positioned under the tail, where the bird's bottom should be.

"We pop this in here, wind it up, whip the key out, give the plane a good push, and off we go," Lisle explained. "The levers inside will help keep us on course. To fly back from the fortress, she just needs to be wound up again and given a shove!"

Mr. Penguin thought that all sounded marvelous, but something was bothering him. He took a closer look at the space for passengers.

"But how are we all going to fit in there?" he asked.

"Oh no," said Edith, "I'd love to go and get Gordon, but there isn't room for us all. Dieter and I are going to stay here and keep watch with the telescope. We'll light a bonfire at the top of the mountain if we need you to come back in a hurry."

That sounded like quite a sensible plan.

Lisle grinned at Mr. Penguin. "That means you, me, and Colin are off to the fortress!"

"I see..." Mr. Penguin gulped. "But who's flying the cuckoo?"

Lisle handed him a pair of goggles.

* * *

A short while later, Mr. Penguin found himself sitting in the pilot's seat of the cuckoo plane. Lisle was quickly running through the flying instructions with him. A fierce and icy wind howled all around them, and Lisle had to shout. They were at the top of one of the steepest roads in the village. It ran straight through the town square and finished, rather terrifyingly, at the end of a small cliff with a sheer drop to the valley below it. Lisle thought this road would make an excellent runway for the plane.

Mr. Penguin thought he might barf into his satchel.

"OK?" Lisle said eventually, smiling.

Mr. Penguin hadn't heard a word of her instructions, but he nodded anyway. Beside him, Colin's eyes gleamed with the bright, giddy shine of someone who thought that this outrageous, dangerous, and bonkers thing they were about to do sounded like the most wonderfully relaxing way to spend an evening.

"I'll be right behind you," yelled Lisle against the wind. "I'll be ready to wind her up again midflight should we need to give her a bit more OOMPH!"

Mr. Penguin nodded again. He'd have liked to have said something very brave and confident—the sort of thing Butch Peril always said in his books before a dangerous mission. But he was trying to keep his breakfast and midafternoon snack firmly in his tummy. He really wanted to run back to the bakery and hide under one of the twins' beds (preferably Dieter's as it was a lot tidier) but the thought of Gordon, kidnapped and all alone, stopped him. He HAD to be rescued.

Mr. Penguin swallowed hard and adjusted his bow tie.

Lisle wound up the cuckoo plane's bottom, then gave Edith and Dieter a nod. They removed the two heavy blocks in front of the wheels, and Edith set the

propeller whirring. Then she
and Dieter gave the machine an
almighty shove and…

WHOOSH!

Off they
went, rattling down
the street! Mr. Penguin,
Colin, and Lisle shuddered and
jittered about. The wind slapped angrily
at their cheeks, and their teeth chitter-
chattered in their mouths and beak.

THIS IS AMAZING!!!!!! said Colin's pad. He was grinning madly beside Mr. Penguin's right flipper, his eyes watering with delight.

Lisle hooted and hollered, yelling, "HERE WE GO!"

And just like that, Mr. Penguin, Colin, and Lisle found themselves flying off a cliff through the air in the tiny cuckoo plane.

CHAPTER SEVENTEEN

YET ANOTHER BUMPY LANDING

M r. Penguin squeezed his eyes shut and tried to ignore the fierce wind whooshing all around him. On his shoulder, Colin was grinning madly. He glanced behind him then tapped Mr. Penguin's forehead.

"I'M NOT LOOKING AT ANY-THING UNTIL WE HAVE LANDED,

COLIN!" yelped Mr. Penguin. But Colin kept tapping until Mr. Penguin had no choice but to open his eyes. Colin pointed his leg back toward the village. A knot of residents stood and watched them go, including Edith and Dieter, who were jumping up and down and waving encouragingly. Then Mr. Penguin saw what had caught Colin's eye.

The mysterious stranger in black stood in the shadow of a King Ludvig von Clonker statue. He was just as Colin had described—sinister and creepy. As Mr. Penguin watched, the man took one last look at the cuckoo plane and then disappeared into the gloom with a swish of his leather coat.

Mr. Penguin groaned. Not only was he

flying into goodness-knew-what peril at the fortress, but he'd also left two of his friends in danger!

It was at this point that Mr. Penguin made the mistake of looking down. Ooh! They were high! So far, in fact, that they were even above the clouds with only the large and icy tip of the Old Grandfather Grimm mountain for company. Mr. Penguin clamped his eyes shut again.

"Mr. Penguin!" cried Lisle. "We need to land! Pull the lever!"

But poor Mr. Penguin couldn't pull anything. His flippers were frozen stiff with terror!

The cuckoo plane smashed into a clump of frozen trees and Bump! Bump! Bumped down through the branches.

CRUNCH!

It hit the ground and chucked its passengers out most impolitely. They tumbled across the snow before coming to an abrupt (and slightly ouchy!) stop against a boulder.

TH-WACK!

Mr. Penguin stood up first and straightened his bow tie. His head was all wobbly and spinning.

"Oh dear! Oh dear! Oh dear!" he cried, glancing over at the cuckoo plane. "We won't be able to get back to the village! Look! It's ruined!"

As they looked at it, one of the wings broke off, the propeller crumpled, and one of the eyelids started doing a weird wink-twitch thing again.

Mr. Penguin waddled around in circles, flapping his flippers and groaning miserably. He only stopped when Colin lobbed a frozen pinecone at him.

Lisle stood next to the wrecked mechanical bird and eyed it up calmly. "This isn't good," she said, "but I *might* be able to fix it. I'll *have* to if we ever want to get home."

She rummaged around in the plane's

bottom and pulled out a little toolbox.

"It's a good job I packed this!" she said. "I'll stay here and get fixing. You two will have to go to the fortress without me."

Mr. Penguin gulped. He wasn't sure what was more worrying—being trapped on this freezing mountain, or facing whatever was inside.

"Go on!" insisted Lisle, rolling up her sleeves. "It's getting dark, and we don't want to be stuck out here for the night—we might be gobbled up by ferocious beasts!"

As Mr. Penguin fussed with his bow tie again, an image of Gordon in his hamster costume flashed into his mind. His friend was probably feeling frightened too.

"OK!" he said. "Let's go!"

* * *

The climb to the fortress was very steep. There was nothing left of the ancient path, and the snow came up to Mr. Penguin's bow tie, so Colin kung fu kicked—KAPOW!—a track up the mountain.

"Thank goodness you're here!" Mr. Penguin said through his chattering beak. "Otherwise I'd be really stuck!"

A blizzard began swirling around them. It was like being shaken in a snow globe as they tried to trundle upward. But then the storm stopped and suddenly the fortress was revealed—a monstrous, weather-beaten building with an enormous, black iron door looming above them.

DOESN'T LOOK LIKE IT'S VERY WELCOMING IF YOU ASK ME, said Colin's pad.

"I agree," said Mr. Penguin, shivering.

LOOKS VERY DANGEROUS

Mr. Penguin nodded.

VERY DANGEROUS INDEED, said Colin's pad.

Then, without breaking eye contact with Mr. Penguin, Colin slowly underlined the word "VERY" with a thick black line.

"All right, Colin!" said Mr. Penguin. "No need to go on about it."

Mr. Penguin waddled slowly up the crumbling steps. Colin stashed his pad away and followed. With a trembling flipper, Mr. Penguin knocked on the door.

No answer.

"Oh dear!" he said, cheerfully. "Looks like no one is at home, so we'll just get Lisle and fly back to the village! Come on!"

And he turned and ran back down the steps.

But Colin wasn't going to be beaten by something as silly as a heavy, definitely reinforced, solid iron door. He furrowed his unibrow, took a deep breath, and... KAPOW!

There was a dreadful clanging sound, and the door opened with an ominous groan. It hadn't been locked!

Curiosity got the better of Mr. Penguin, and he found himself climbing back up the steps.

"How strange," he whispered. "If you were up to no good, why on earth would you leave the front door unlocked? Anyone could just wander in."

Little did he know that he was just about to find out in a VERY alarming way.

My plan is simple. I am going to take over the world.

I spent my childhood performing for the rich and the powerful, and now I think it's high time they performed for me. How thrilling it will be to have everybody under my spell, doing my bidding forever!

CHAPTER EIGHTEEN

THE MOVING FLOOR

Just as Mr. Penguin and Colin crept through the door, a sudden blast of howling wind slammed it shut behind them. Somewhere in the darkness above them, there was the clunk of a deadbolt dropping into place and Mr. Penguin trembled—they were now locked inside the fortress!

It was pitch-black at first, but slowly Mr. Penguin's eyes became accustomed to the dark.

He saw they were standing at the top of a set of stone steps that led down to a cavernous hall. It was icy cold in the room and had they been able to see properly, they'd have noticed their breath billowing from their mouths.

Mr. Penguin squinted. Something on the

far side of the hall seemed to be glowing. He squeezed his eyes almost completely shut and could just make out another door with a yellowy-green light spilling through the cracks around the door frame.

"I think we need to head over there," Mr. Penguin whispered, pointing with a flipper.

Colin nodded, and they walked down the steps together toward the glowing light. Mr. Penguin was first to set foot on the ground, but he quickly jumped back onto the last step. The floor of the entrance hall was springy and rubbery! What on earth was it? He could hear a gentle hissing sound coming from somewhere nearby, like someone had turned a tap on.

Surely some mad person wasn't standing in the darkness turning on taps?

I mean, I like a nice hot bath… thought Mr. Penguin, scratching his beak. *But not in a terrifying fortress up a mountain in the middle of the blizzard with no lights on. I wouldn't be able to find my rubber duckie…*

He shook himself and remembered they were here to rescue their friend, and hopefully all the stolen rodents too. It was a very important rescue mission! Mr. Penguin straightened his nice hat and tried walking on the floor again.

This time, the ground hissed angrily and started to slither and move all around his ankles. Mr. Penguin leapt back beside Colin.

He gulped.

Just then, a shaft of moonlight slipped through one of the windows and lit up a knife-thin slice of the room. Mr. Penguin could finally make out what was beneath him.

There wasn't a mad person running a bath.

Oh no! It was something worse.

Much worse.

The entire floor was covered with slithery SNAKES, all hissing and wiggling about very angrily. There were small snakes, big snakes, and some snakes so gigantic they looked as if they'd be able to swallow Mr. Penguin in one big gulp!

"S…S…S…SNAKES!" cried Mr. Penguin as he and Colin hoofed it back up the steps.

"Am I still alive?!" said Mr. Penguin, one flipper clamped to his forehead. "Have I been eaten?"

Colin didn't answer. He was too busy examining the object that had trapped his friend. He grinned.

AHA! said his pad.

And then:

OF COURSE.

He turned to Mr. Penguin, and Colin's pad said:

CHAPTER NINETEEN

ANOTHER CUNNING DISGUISE

I don't think this is going to work!" whispered Mr. Penguin, five minutes later. "I don't think this is going to work AT ALL."

Colin rolled his eyes. His pad said:

IT IS THE ONLY WAY OF GETTING OUT WITHOUT BEING GOBBLED UP.

Mr. Penguin made some very worried sort of noises.

AND IF YOU CAN'T KEEP QUIET AT LEAST SAY "HISSSSSS."

Next page:

WE ARE MEANT TO BE A SNAKE.

The object that had trapped Mr. Penguin was the dry skin that one of the bigger snakes had shed.

Colin had remembered when he and Mr. Penguin had gone promenading around the Cityville Zoo one day and had stumbled upon a very clever zookeeper doing an interesting talk in the reptile house. Apparently, every so often a snake finds itself feeling a bit twitchy and itchy, and then it slithers out of its skin to reveal a brand new layer of shimmering scaly skin beneath.

(Mr. Penguin hadn't heard one word of this because he'd tripped while eating an ice cream and had splodged it all down a very large, well-dressed lady. He'd been too busy trying to clean it off her with his bow tie before she noticed.)

And now they were in the fortress wiggling through the slithery snakes in their snake costume.

Mr. Penguin tried his best not to be nervous and did his best HISSSSSSSS-ing, and they soon reached the steps to the glowing door. But now wiggling was no good—they needed to run.

They threw off their disguise and scampered up the steps, but several of the larger snakes realized they'd been tricked and snapped at Mr. Penguin's brogues with their hefty-looking fangs. Colin pulled his friend out of harm's way while biffing them on their noses.

Eventually they made it to the top step, and they were safe. Mr. Penguin pushed open the door, and they scurried into the room, shutting the snakes behind them.

They were now in a vast, round chamber with damp stone walls. The glowing yellowy-green light was coming from several lamps that flickered and fizzed around the room.

Mr. Penguin glanced around. "It looks like a workshop…" he whispered.

Colin agreed with him, but he was still feeling very suspicious, so he just wrote:

MMMMMMMMM... on his pad and continued snooping.

The room was even messier than Lisle's workroom behind the von Clonker clock. Cogs and wheels and sheets of gleaming metal littered the floor. There were desks scattered with dangerous-looking tools, and the walls were covered in huge pieces of paper scribbled with complicated equations and plans.

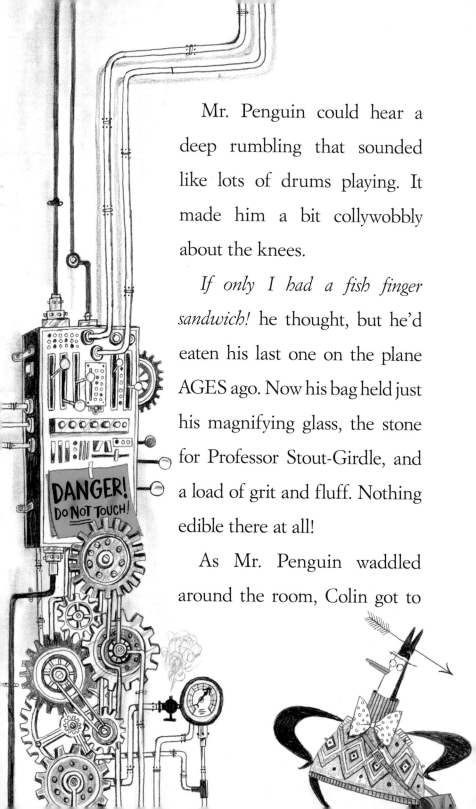

Mr. Penguin could hear a deep rumbling that sounded like lots of drums playing. It made him a bit collywobbly about the knees.

If only I had a fish finger sandwich! he thought, but he'd eaten his last one on the plane AGES ago. Now his bag held just his magnifying glass, the stone for Professor Stout-Girdle, and a load of grit and fluff. Nothing edible there at all!

As Mr. Penguin waddled around the room, Colin got to

DANGER! DO NOT TOUCH!

work. He leapt up onto the desks to see if he could find anything useful.

"What can it all be for?" said Mr. Penguin, peering at a strange-looking instrument that was sparking dangerously. There was a row of blinking buttons above a sign that said: DANGER! Do not touch!

Whenever Mr. Penguin saw a sign like that all he wanted to do was touch everything, immediately. He actually had to hold one flipper back with the other one to stop himself.

Colin, meanwhile, had found something—an old, rather tatty notebook. It looked both interesting *and* important. He wrote something to try to catch Mr. Penguin's attention.

AHEM! said his pad.

"I mean, how did all this stuff get here?" continued Mr. Penguin, talking to himself. "Do you think we might be facing an evil robot or something?"

Colin tried to get his attention again.

AHEM!

No luck. Mr. Penguin was now twirling about in the middle of the room, flippers on hips, looking at everything.

"If ONLY there was a clue some-where—something *extremely* detailed that could tell us what was going on and who's behind it all."

Colin sighed on his pad, tucked the notebook under his arms, scuttled over to Mr. Penguin, and schlonked him on the ankle with it.

"Steady on, Colin!" exclaimed Mr. Penguin. "What is it? I was just saying—if only—"

Catching sight of the words on the front of the notebook, he gasped. Very carefully, Mr. Penguin took the book from Colin and studied it.

On the grubby front cover, scribbled in the same handwriting as the notes on the walls, were these words:

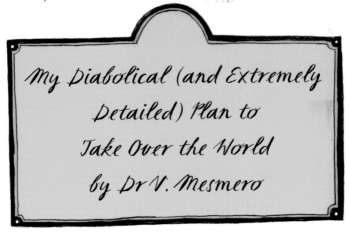

My Diabolical (and Extremely Detailed) Plan to Take Over the World by Dr V. Mesmero

It was EXACTLY the sort of clue they needed!

With trembling flippers Mr. Penguin flicked open the book, and the two chums started to read from the beginning:

My name is Dr. Mesmero, and I am a hypnotist. Actually, I am absolutely and without any doubt the best hypnotist in the world.

Mr. Penguin and Colin read as quickly as they could, their eyes flicking over the words, Mr. Penguin's flippers a blur as they turned the pages. They read all about Dr. Mesmero's childhood, the trademark dark glasses, and the audiences that came to see the famous hypnotist. At last they reached the most important part.

A Diabolical Plan

Stage 1

I have invented a machine called The Hypnotron, that can hypnotize thousands of people at once by using the hypnotic rays from my eyes. With it I will ensnare every person and creature in the whole world in my hypnotic web.

Over the last year I have installed reflector dishes on monuments around the globe: the Pyramids, the Great Wall in the Distant East, and the tallest buildings in the busiest cities. Even in the Frozen South and the Frozen North! It sounds like I worked really hard, but it was actually very easy. I just hypnotized every person I met along the way, and they did all the work whilst I watched with giddy glee knowing one day everyone on earth would be under my control.

Stage 2

Next I had to decide where The Hypnotron should be placed for maximum impact. It needed to be on top of a tall mountain, but where? And how would I power it? Generally mountains, especially the very tallest ones, are not connected to electricity. Then the answer to both problems came in one package.

I was flicking through a newspaper in Cityville whilst supervising the installation of a reflector dish on the tallest sky-scraper. The main story was a boring one about how some idiotic penguin and his spider friend had found some treasure in a museum or something. But next to this story was a small advert for the 32nd Rodent Games to be held in the mountain town of Schneedorf-on-the-Peak.

I went to the Cityville library and discovered that Schneedorf is one of the highest inhabited places in the world. The mountain is only overshadowed literally by the mountain next door to it—Old Grandfather Grimm. The location was perfect. I read there was even an abandoned fortress I could use to house The Hypnotron!

But how would I power it? Well, the answer was also there, in the newspaper—by using the rodents gathered on the neighboring mountain for the Rodent Games! I remembered the pet hamster I'd had as a child and how she would spend hours running like mad in her exercise wheel. If I could harness the energy created by hundreds of rodents doing that, I would be able to create enough energy to power The Hypnotron.

Stage 3

I packed everything I needed into the large basket of a hot air balloon, which I'd stolen from a hypnotized balloon enthusiast. Then silently, under cover of darkness, I flew up the mountain and began to build my machine inside the fortress.

Stage 4

Next I needed the rodents from Schneedorf. But I wouldn't be able to sneak over to the village in my hot air balloon—I'd soon be noticed. And the winds howling around this mountain could easily blow the balloon off course.

The answer came when I explored the basement of this freezing dump and found it to be FULL of snakes. Pets of the previous owner, I guessed, that had been left to multiply and adapt to the freezing conditions over the last two hundred years.

After a quick blast of my hypnotic eyes, they were under my command. I instructed them to steal the rodents from the village and bring them to me. They did this by wiggling through a network of ancient drainage pipes that connect the fortress to the village.

Everything has now fallen into place, and I am ready to put my diabolical plan into action.

CHAPTER TWENTY

CAUGHT
RED-FLIPPERED!

Mr. Penguin shut the notebook and gulped. YIKES! Whatever he thought might have been going on in the fortress, he never imagined it would be as mad and as dangerous as this!

Even Colin, who was never really rattled by anything, looked a bit green under his unibrow.

Mr. Penguin and Colin stood blinking at each other. What were they going to do? They were up against someone who was both completely bonkers *and* utterly dastardly.

A sudden noise in the chamber made them jump. Behind them, a concealed door in the wall of the chamber (that had been pretending to be an enormous inglenook fireplace) swung open.

"Well...well...well. What *do* we have here?" snarled a voice that didn't sound at all like it was going to offer them a nice cup of tea and a dunky biscuit.

Mr. Penguin and Colin swizzled around on the spot. Someone was standing in the hidden entrance, silhouetted against a harsh electric light.

CHAPTER TWENTY-ONE

AN APPOINTMENT WITH THE DOCTOR

The stranger in black! thought Mr. Penguin with a tremble. *It's him!*

But it wasn't him.

In fact, it wasn't a him at all...

The clip-clop of heels echoed around the chamber as a woman stalked out from the hidden entrance, slamming the door shut behind her.

She had blond ringlets, and her face was heavily covered in makeup, with two bright pink circles on her cheeks and a spattering of painted-on freckles. Her mouth was a bright red slash that was smiling, but not in a happy, cheerful way.

"She looks like she's never eaten a fish finger sandwich in her *entire* life," thought Mr. Penguin, continuing to ogle her. The woman was wearing what looked like an old stage costume—a frilly, satin dress that was slightly too small for her and covered in dirty splodges of engine oil. Her eyes were hidden behind a pair of thick sunglasses.

"Who are you? What are you doing here?" she hissed.

"Er...er..." spluttered Mr. Penguin.

"We were just um…"

TIDYING, said Colin's pad.

"Yes!" said Mr. Penguin. "TIDYING! Look!"

To prove his point, he carefully moved a pencil on the desk in front of him so it lined up neatly with another. Then he smiled his best beaky smile.

The woman opened her mouth to say something, but instead she suddenly shrieked.

"My dastardly plan!" she yelled, spotting her notebook tucked under Mr. Penguin's flipper. "So you've read all about it, have you?"

Dr. Mesmero leaned toward Mr. Penguin and Colin and peered at them from behind her dark glasses.

"Wait...I know you," she muttered. "I've seen you before..."

She grinned a crocodile-like grin. "Well...if it isn't the famous Adventurer and Penguin, Mr. Penguin. And his little friend the spider too!" she cried.

Colin held up his pad:

HELLO MY NAME IS COLIN.

"I've read all about you!" she said. "In the Cityville newspaper!"

She folded her arms and continued to glare at her visitors. "Let me guess—you've come here to try to stop me from taking over the world?" She snorted. "You'll never succeed! Now give me my book!"

Mr. Penguin hid her notebook behind his back and puffed his chest out.

"Never!" he said. "We've come to rescue our friend Gordon and all the other animals you've stolen!" (Even though he'd wanted to say it in a very brave sort of voice, it came out all wobbly like a jelly.)

"I see," said Dr. Mesmero, and she went to snatch the book, but—

RUN MR. PENGUIN! said Colin's pad. Mr. Penguin didn't need telling twice. He ducked away from Dr. Mesmero, and he and Colin set off.

They ran around the room in circles, with Dr. Mesmero chasing—round and round, first one way, then the other. This went on for approximately ten minutes until

CHAPTER TWENTY-ONE

Dr. Mesmero stopped on one side of the room, and the Adventurers on the other.

"This is ridiculous!" she said, and she clapped her hands.

The hidden door swung open again, and two very long, very hypnotized snakes wiggled into the room.

"SEIZE THEM!" cried Dr. Mesmero.

Before Mr. Penguin and Colin could move, the snakes had zipped across the room and wrapped themselves around the Adventurers like living, slithery ropes.

Mr. Penguin and Colin were trapped!

CHAPTER TWENTY-TWO

TIME FOR DINNER?

N ow..." mused Dr. Mesmero, "what *am* I going to do with you both? Tonight is the night that I take over the world, and I cannot have my great project interrupted!"

She glanced over to Mr. Penguin and Colin. Only their eyes peeked out between the coils of the snakes holding them.

"I could hypnotize you," she continued, "but I need to reserve my power for The Hypnotron."

She thought for a moment, then she nodded.

"Yes, there's nothing else for it," she said. "I'll feed you to the snakes. They'll gobble you up immediately."

Mr. Penguin squeaked from inside his snake prison. Colin squeezed two of his legs out to hold up his pad.

It said NO THANK YOU

Dr. Mesmero ignored him and clicked her fingers at the snakes.

"Take them next door!" she commanded. Mr. Penguin and Colin found themselves being bumped along the ground back toward the hall of snakes.

Then they heard, "WAIT!"

Mr. Penguin peeked out and saw Dr. Mesmero standing in the middle of the room with a fizzing lamp shining directly on her like a spotlight. "This is my big night," she whispered to herself now. "And I always DID perform best in front of a crowd. It would be a shame not to have an audience for the grand finale of my plan…"

She turned to Mr. Penguin and Colin and grinned a toothy grin. Colin held his notepad toward Mr. Penguin. It said YIKES!

And Mr. Penguin had to agree.

"You'll soon see just how powerful I am! Afterward, you will make a nice midnight snack for the snakes. It will be a fulfilling evening for both them and me."

She clicked her fingers again and turned toward the hidden door. The two snakes followed, dragging Mr. Penguin and Colin along the floor.

"This isn't going to do my nice Adventurer's hat any good at all," tutted Mr. Penguin. "And I bet my satchel is getting all scuffed up…"

They traveled down a cold and cobwebby tunnel behind Dr. Mesmero's clip-clopping heels. The drip, drip, drip of icy water falling from the ceiling was joined by a great thundering noise that grew louder and louder.

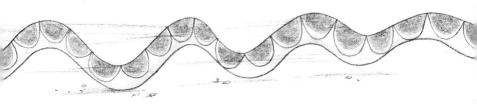

They reached a fireplace at the end of the secret tunnel. Mr. Penguin was worried that he might be pulled up through the chimney when the fireplace swung around like a revolving hotel lobby door. It opened out into a large chamber with a polished stone floor and a high, domed ceiling. The thundering noise was deafeningly loud now, and Mr. Penguin and Colin could see what was causing it. If Mr. Penguin had been a goose, it would have made him go pimply all over.

All around the edge of the chamber were hundreds of hamster cages stacked one on top of another, forming a strange sort of wall around the room. They were all filled with rodents running like crazy in their exercise wheels—making the groaning noise that shook the room. But while their little legs were scampering, their eyes were blank and swirling. They'd been hypnotized!

Mr. Penguin's eyes swiveled around to look for Gordon. Where was he?

AHA! There! He was the only creature not running at high speed. Still in his hamster costume, he took a few steps on his wheel then flew around it on his bottom before falling out onto the sawdust of his cage. Then he picked himself up and did it all over again. He seemed to be thoroughly enjoying himself and completely unaware that he was in Absolute Danger.

Mr. Penguin saw that all the cages were connected by a thick black cable that ran across the floor to a giant, humming metal box. From that, a gigantic cable—wider than Mr. Penguin's entire head—wiggled across the floor and plugged into a monstrous machine in the middle of the chamber. It gleamed in the strange green-yellow light and pointed straight up at the domed roof.

The doctor grinned a wide, wolfish grin.

"BEHOLD," she cried loudly over the rumbling noise, "THE HYPNOTRON!"

CHAPTER TWENTY-THREE

THE FINAL CURTAIN

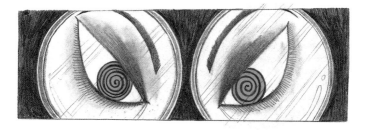

Wonderful, isn't it?" continued Dr. Mesmero. She patted its shiny metal sides. "My life's work!"

She strode around the room like a ringmaster in a circus.

"This mountain is the perfect location for my machine," she cried, as if she were addressing an enormous audience. "From here, my hypnotic beams will reach all around the world and, within a matter of minutes, everything will be under my control."

She paused dramatically.

"…to take over the world!"

She bowed several times, and Mr. Penguin wondered if she could hear the applause of an invisible audience. Then she leapt straight to work, fiddling with knobs, pulling levers, and adjusting a pair of what looked like binoculars attached to one end of the machine.

When she was happy with the goggles, Dr. Mesmero stalked across the room and yanked on a huge lever on the wall. The sound of rusty metal creaking echoed around the chamber and the domed ceiling started opening to the sky. Freezing air swirled snowflakes into the room.

She's going to do it! thought Mr. Penguin,

his flippers trembling again. *She's going to take over the world! We must stop her!*

But how?

Mr. Penguin gritted his beak. He wanted to think nice thoughts about fish finger sandwiches, but they needed a plan. They could pull the power from the machine, but not while they were tightly trussed up by two large snakes with enormous teeth.

As the roof ground to a stop, Dr. Mesmero strode back to The Hypnotron and adjusted its position slightly. Then she sat on the stool by the binoculars and turned to Mr. Penguin and Colin.

"Enjoy the show, boys!" she yelled. "And afterward it's going to be the final curtain for you both!"

She removed her dark glasses to reveal a pair of bright green eyes. She looked into the binoculars and tightened a strap behind her head.

Dr. Mesmero took a deep breath, and the liquid in a large glass gauge on the side of the machine shot upward. *She must be summoning up her power!* thought Mr. Penguin. The Hypnotron shuddered and hummed loudly. The lights in the chamber started to pulse and flash as all the power in the room was sucked into the machine like dust up a vacuum.

"COLIN!" shouted Mr. Penguin, over the noise. "WE NEED TO DO SOME-THING! CAN YOU GET THESE STINKY SNAKES OFF US?"

A thick, lime-green beam of light suddenly shot out of the far end of The Hypnotron with a horrendous fizzing noise. It cut through the dark sky like a hot knife through butter. Underneath it, The Hypnotron shook violently on its base, and the entire room jerked and juddered.

Colin's eyes darted about as his brain made complicated kung fu equations. Eventually he furrowed his unibrow, gritted his teeth, and nodded.

YES, said his pad.

WHEN I SAY GO!

READY...

Next page:

STEADY...

Next page...

CHAPTER TWENTY-FOUR

LIGHTS AND LASERS

G O! KAPOW! Colin kicked out with all of his legs at once, sending the snake wrapped around him flying across the room. Without stopping for a moment, Colin scampered over to Mr. Penguin, grabbed the other snake by the tail, and tugged hard.

Mr. Penguin turbo-twirled on the spot as the snake rapidly uncoiled. Colin then swung it above his head and lobbed it across the room. Mr. Penguin was free! Dizzy, but free! And the two bamboozled serpents took one last googly-eyed look at Colin then skedaddled away through the fireplace door.

"EXCELLENT WORK, COLIN!" said Mr. Penguin, straightening his nice Adventurer's hat. "NOW WE NEED TO UNPLUG THE HYPNOTRON!"

Mr. Penguin, with Colin hot on his heels, waddled over to the cables that ran into the big metal box. They gathered up as many of the thick wires as they could and pulled hard.

HEEEEAAAAVE!

But nothing happened.

They tried again. Nothing. The cables were fixed tight.

A more drastic plan was needed.

Colin leapt into action, swinging himself toward the box and kicking it.

KAPOW! KAPOW! But it wouldn't budge. He took a deep breath, summoned up all his kung fu power, and head-butted it—CLONK—but all that did was dent the metal a bit.

HEAVE!

Mr. Penguin started to do his panicky dance again, waddling about and flapping his flippers and yelping, "Oh dear! Oh dear! Oh dear! What are we going to do?"

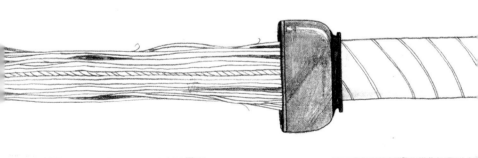

The two Adventurers looked around for something to throw at The Hypnotron. They needed a rock or a wrench or a tool of some kind—anything chuckable—but there was nothing useful lying around at all. Compared to Dr. Mesmero's workshop, this room was terribly tidy.

As he turned, Mr. Penguin caught sight of the satchel on his back. His magnifying glass! He could throw that!

He whipped it out of his satchel and looked at it sadly. What if it got broken? Colin rolled his eyes, snatched it from

Mr. Penguin's flipper, and hurled it at the machine. It clanged against it and—

—bounced off and slid under one of the cages. MISSED! Now it was lost, and they still hadn't stopped the machine!

"Colin?" hollered Mr. Penguin, wild-eyed. "Can I throw you?"

Scribblings.

NO THANK YOU, said the pad.

Mr. Penguin ferreted about in his satchel for something else to chuck, and his flipper found the stone they'd rescued on the hotel rooftop!

Did he dare? What would Professor Stout-Girdle say if Mr. Penguin handed her a broken stone when he got back to Cityville? She probably wouldn't give them any money as a reward, so there would probably be no fish finger sandwiches… But he had to save the world from the bonkers Dr. Mesmero. There was nothing else for it.

Mr. Penguin held the heavy stone in one flipper, eyed his target and—WHOOOOSH—threw it hard at the devilish machine.

CLONK!

It hit the machine with an almighty clang, then bounced across the room and landed with a thump. It hadn't stopped the cogs inside, but The Hypnotron was now swinging around on its base. The hypnotic beam was no longer pointing up into the sky, but spinning wildly about inside the chamber.

It made PEW! PEW! noises as it blasted great holes in the walls.

Dr. Mesmero ripped off her binoculars.

"WHAT ARE YOU DOING?" she snarled angrily, as the room filled with smoke and rubble. "You are ruining my plan!"

Before Mr. Penguin could think of a witty answer, the hypnotic beam swung around and fired at the stone. Something extraordinary happened. The rock wasn't blasted to smithereens but split open like an Easter egg. Inside, an enormous and very beautiful diamond sparkled in the green light.

Mr. Penguin gasped and so did Colin on his pad:

GASP!

The beam hit the sparkling surface of the diamond, which, like a mirror, reflected it back. It zinged across the room and blasted Dr. Mesmero right in the face, sending her flying.

As Mr. Penguin and Colin ducked, the machine kept on spinning wildly, and the beam hit the cable box that Mr. Penguin and Colin had tried to open moments before. There was a terrifying buzzing noise.

The floor shook.

Colin held his breath.

Mr. Penguin held onto his hat.

More smoke filled the room, then the cable box and The Hypnotron exploded with an almighty, earth-shuddering BANG!

CHAPTER TWENTY-FIVE

THE GREAT ESCAPE

BANG!

M r. Penguin sat up on a pile of rubble and dusted off his hat. It was looking a bit battered about the edges, but thankfully it would be OK. His ears were buzzing like an angry wasps' nest, and he was covered in dirt.

Colin clambered out from behind some broken bricks and handed Mr. Penguin the gigantic diamond he'd recovered.

Holding it in his flippers, Mr. Penguin marveled at the gigantic gem. Even in the smoke-filled room, it seemed to sparkle

and shine with a light that seemed to come from within. *It must be worth a fortune!* Mr. Penguin thought. And he'd been wandering around with it in his bag! He stashed the diamond away along with his magnifying glass that Colin had pulled out from under a cage. It now had a huge crack across the glass.

"What do we do now?" Mr. Penguin asked Colin. His beak was dry and dusty, and his voice came out all croaky like a frog's. He wanted a nice cup of tea, a fish finger sandwich, and a good sleep in his hammock back in his Cityville igloo, but that was completely impossible at the moment.

WE NEED TO GET OUT! said Colin's pad, and Mr. Penguin agreed.

But how? They'd have to pick their way out of this rubble to find Lisle. Mr. Penguin doubted she'd been able to fix the cuckoo plane. He'd made a dreadful mess of it when he'd crashed it, so it looked as if they would be stuck up this mountain FOREVER.

He groaned loudly and hid his entire head down the neck of his sweater, wishing someone else was there to sort out all this kerfuffle.

Then he heard the hidden door in the fireplace creak and felt Colin poke him on the belly. Mr. Penguin groaned again. Whatever was happening, he wasn't sure he had the energy to face it. He burrowed even farther down inside his sweater.

"Is he OK?" asked a voice.

Mr. Penguin's head shot out from his sweater.

"Lisle!" he cried, and he sat up and gave his friend a hearty hug about the knees. Beside him, Colin was scribbling away on his pad. It said HE'S FINE. HE'S JUST HAVING ONE OF HIS MOMENTS.

But Mr. Penguin didn't see that—he was too excited to see Lisle! She was covered in smudgy oil stains and standing with her hands on her hips.

"How did you get here?" asked Mr. Penguin.

"I heard all the odd noises coming from the fortress and thought I'd better hoof it up here to see if you were OK!" she explained.

"But the snakes?" said Mr. Penguin, wide-eyed. "Did they bite you?"

Lisle laughed. "No, not at all!" she cried. "Quite the opposite in fact! I found the front door locked, but then discovered a little old rotten wooden door at the back of the fortress, covered in snow. As I tugged it open, snakes came shooting out like deflating birthday balloons—all looking terrified. They slithered off, and didn't even look at me!"

Mr. Penguin was very relieved and, at nine hundred miles per hour, he told her everything that had happened since they'd left her.

"We're VERY glad to see you!" he said once he'd finished. "Did you manage to fix the cuckoo plane?"

Lisle's brow crinkled.

"No, I'm afraid," she said sadly. "It's too badly broken. I wondered if there might be a plane here in the fortress we could escape in, but I haven't seen one…"

Her voice trailed away. Mr. Penguin groaned again. They really were trapped on the mountain. He hoped Edith and the people of Schneedorf-on-the-Peak would organize a rescue mission, but that could take DAYS, and his stomach was already turning itself upside down and inside out with hunger.

"The only thing I *did* find was an enormous basket thing covered in a sheet. That was just before I heard the explosion and came running to see if you were OK."

"A basket covered in a sheet? That isn't helpful at all," thought Mr. Penguin. "Now isn't the time for a picnic!"

But out came Colin's pad.

I THINK THAT MIGHT BE A HOT AIR BALLOON, it said.

Mr. Penguin snapped his flippers. Of course! Dr. Mesmero hadn't used a plane to get here—she'd snuck up silently one night in a hot air balloon!

Mr. Penguin leapt up and did a little dance of happiness on the rubble. They were saved! But his giddiness didn't last long.

A great blast of wind rattled around the chamber, toppling bricks from the roof into the room. A large crack zigzagged down one of the walls, and what remained of the roof started to quiver above them.

"Quick!" said Lisle. "We need to leave pronto before this whole place falls down around us! I'll get the balloon inflated, you get all the hamsters!" She darted off, hurdling over bricks and machinery before disappearing back down the tunnel behind the fireplace.

The hamsters! Gordon! In all of the

explosions and excitement, Mr. Penguin
had almost, but not quite, forgotten them.
He jumped to his feet and waddled over to
the cages, wafting away the smoke with his
flippers. All the hamsters were blinking in
a stunned fashion. Whatever hypnotic spell
they'd been under, it had been broken.
They looked around them, trying to make

sense of where they were and what they were doing. Everyone except Gordon. He was still trying to work out how to use the exercise wheel and falling off it every few seconds.

Mr. Penguin reached in and pulled his friend out. He gave him a quick hug. "Silly old pigeon!" he said, and he popped

Gordon on top of his head where he knew he'd feel at home.

Then Mr. Penguin and Colin unlocked all the cages and helped the rodents out. They got them lined up nice and orderly behind Colin, ready to scamper off to the hot air balloon. They looked like they were going on a school trip. Mr. Penguin took Gordon from his head and tucked him safely under his flipper, just in case he decided to go flapping back to his cage.

LET'S GO, said Colin's pad, but Mr. Penguin was dithering and shuffling his feet.

? said Colin's pad.

Mr. Penguin nibbled his beak. "It's Dr. Mesmero..." he said. "We shouldn't just leave her here. She could be hurt..."

BUT THE ROOF IS GOING TO FALL ON OUR HEADS AT ANY MOMENT!

Colin scribbled on his pad while trying to stop a hamster from chewing the end of his pen.

"I'll be two flaps of a flipper!" said Mr. Penguin.

After some waddling about and shifting of things (he found Dr. Mesmero's notebook under a tangle of fizzing wires and stashed it away in his satchel), he discovered Dr. Mesmero sitting against a wall, staring into space. Her blond hair stood bolt upright and her face was covered in thick black dust.

"Um…Are you OK, Dr. Mesmero?" said Mr. Penguin.

No answer, so he tapped her on the head with a flipper.

Then he waggled a flipper in front of her face. She still didn't respond.

She didn't even blink!

Then Mr. Penguin noticed the faint swirls in her eyes. "Great tuna steaks!" he cried. "She's hypnotized herself! It must have happened when The Hypnotron beam bounced off the diamond and walloped her directly in the phizog!"

Well, thought Mr. Penguin, *I definitely can't leave her here! She'll turn into a block of ice in minutes—that's if the roof doesn't fall in and clonk her on the head first.*

Mr. Penguin wasn't sure what he would do with her once they got back to the village, but he was bringing her with him anyway.

Mr. Penguin cleared his throat and said in his best, most sensible voice: "FOLLOW ME!" And like magic, she did! She'd do whatever he wanted! He shuddered. That might sound fun, but he knew that sort of power was incredibly dangerous—especially in the hands of people like Dr. Mesmero.

He led her across the room and down the tunnel. Lisle had inflated the hot air balloon, and Colin was helping the last of the rescued rodents into the basket, looking very sternly at the giddy ones jostling at the back.

Mr. Penguin sat Dr. Mesmero down in a corner of the basket, and Lisle untied the ropes holding the balloon to the ground. As gracefully as a basket full of rodents, two humans, a spider, and a rather portly penguin with a pigeon dressed as a hamster tucked under his arm could move, the Adventurers rose into the air and floated gently across the valley to safety.

They were hardly above the clouds when, down below them, the whole of the fortress roof fell in and the entire building crumbled to dust.

CHAPTER TWENTY-SIX

A SURPRISE AT THE HAUS OF STRUDEL

As the hot air balloon started its slow descent, quite a crowd gathered in the town square.

Mr. Penguin offered to help Lisle and Colin land the balloon, but after their experience of him piloting the cuckoo plane, they politely refused.

As soon as they touched the ground, Mr. Penguin swung open the little door and all the rodents ran out of the basket and scurried to meet their owners. Mr. Penguin stood watching the lovely scene with his chest puffed out and his flippers on his hips as excited squeaks filled the air and everyone petted and nose-kissed their furry friends.

All except two.

Gordon stood blinking with one eye and then the other, as usual. The second creature was a little hamster with funny, sticky-up sort of fur all around his bottom. He looked a bit bewildered and lost.

"Colonel Tuftybum!" exclaimed Lisle. She scooped him up and gave him a little tickle behind the ears, which he thoroughly enjoyed.

"This is Dieter's hamster," said Lisle, looking around anxiously for her brother. "But where is he?"

Mr. Penguin's jolly feeling turned gray and cloudy. His tummy flipped upside down, and he felt like he'd swallowed a rock. Something wasn't right. Where WAS Dieter? And Edith? They should have been the very first people to welcome them home. Mr. Penguin knew Edith had been very worried about Gordon.

So if they weren't there…

SOMETHING IS WRONG, said Colin's pad.

"Maybe they are still asleep at home?" said Lisle, but under her chirpy tone, there was a worried wobble in her voice. "It IS very early still…"

Lisle and Colonel Tuftybum led Mr. Penguin, Colin, Gordon, and the still-hypnotized Dr. Mesmero across the square. Every few steps, delighted people stopped to thank them, clap them on the back, shake Mr. Penguin by the flipper, and eye the strange woman with the dust-covered face and floofy hair. Eventually, the gang made it to the Haus of Strudel.

The lights were off, and all was quiet.

Lisle turned the door handle, but nothing happened. The door was locked!

"Hmmm…" said Lisle. "Maybe they're in the back kitchen. It's warmer there first thing in the morning…"

She led the way down a dark, narrow passage behind the bakery. Mr. Penguin and Colin eyeballed each other. They were both very worried.

The gang clambered across the small, snow-covered yard piled high with empty delivery pallets. Lisle tried the door, but that was locked too. The curtains were drawn, but a faint yellow glow came from inside.

Mr. Penguin squashed his face against the door and had a good ear waggle. He heard hushed voices and the sound of chairs being pushed back across the tiled kitchen floor.

Mr. Penguin's heart hammered in his chest.

Suddenly the door opened and Mr. Penguin found himself face to belly with the mysterious man in black.

CHAPTER TWENTY-SEVEN

THE B.U.M.

Mr. Penguin stood glued to the ground. He looked at the man's long pale face, sinister dark glasses, and grim expression. Then the light glinted off a badge on his lapel, and Mr. Penguin gasped! It matched the one the glamorous

lady had been wearing on the roof of the
Golden Pagoda Hotel. He was part of her
gang!

"RUN!" yelled Mr. Penguin, and he
swiveled on his heels and started to hoof it
across the yard. He didn't get far because he
stepped on the end of a plank of wood that
swung up, walloped him in the face, and
sent him flying, Gordon still under his arm.

Crash!

"COLIN!" cried Mr. Penguin. "QUICK!
BIFF HIM ON THE NOSE! CLONK
HIM ON THE KNEECAP! GIVE HIM
THE WHAT-FOR!"

Colin was just about to put his kung fu
kicking legs into action when a voice floated
out from inside the kitchen.

"Colin, there will be NO nose biffing or knee clonking. Mr. Penguin, come inside IMMEDIATELY."

It was Edith's voice, and her tone told Mr. Penguin not to argue. Colin looked bitterly disappointed.

The man in black reached over and hoisted Mr. Penguin up by his satchel and out of the snow. He placed him gently the right way up, put Mr. Penguin's hat back on his head, and straightened Mr. Penguin's bow tie. Then he stood back politely and gestured for everyone to go into the kitchen in front of him.

What in the name of haddock fillets is happening? thought Mr. Penguin. *Was this strange man in cahoots with Dr. Mesmero?*

Had he hypnotized Edith Hedge? It would take a brave man to try...

Mr. Penguin followed Lisle, Colonel Tuftybum, Dr. Mesmero, and Colin into the bakery. Inside, there was no spine-tingly scene of peril, but something very like a tea party!

Helga was bustling about with a coffee pot, and the whole cozy room smelled of fresh ginger cookies. Edith leapt from her chair by the oven when she saw her friends walk in, Gordon tucked under Mr. Penguin's flipper.

"COLONEL TUFTYBUM!" Dieter cried, appearing from the pantry. He ran across the room and caught his hamster as it jumped squeaking from Lisle's arms.

CHAPTER TWENTY-SEVEN

"Thank goodness you're all safe!" said Helga.

"We've been so worried!" said Edith. She took Gordon from Mr. Penguin, gave him a cuddle, then popped him on her head. "We were just about to launch a rescue mission!"

Helga started to dish out mugs of hot cocoa and swirly cinnamon buns (still no fish fingers or fish paste, Mr. Penguin noticed mournfully), and Lisle began telling everyone the tale. Mr. Penguin explained about the fortress and The Hypnotron and showed everyone Dr. Mesmero's notebook with all her plans written in it. Colin, between swallowing cinnamon buns practically whole, embroidered the story with lots of colorful details.

Edith, Helga, Dieter, and the man in black listened intently, only interrupting to gasp at just the right moments.

When the story was over, everyone started talking at once. Edith fussed over Gordon, Helga fussed over Lisle, Dieter fussed over Colonel Tuftybum, and Colin fussed over the pastries.

Mr. Penguin continued to scoop large portions into his mouth, but he still felt perturbed by the mysterious man in black standing in the corner. Finally, he couldn't hold it in any longer. He stood on his chair and asked, "Please can someone tell me who this person is?" He pointed at the stranger with his flipper. "I'm VERY worried he might be a baddie!"

"A baddie?" Edith hooted. "Not at all, Mr. Penguin. He's here to help! This is Reginald Spy-Glasse. He's from the B.U.M."

"The BUM?" exclaimed Mr. Penguin, and Colin tittered on his pad.

"No, B.U.M.," corrected the man, stepping forward and shaking Mr. Penguin heartily by the flipper. He had a jolly sort of voice, and now his dark glasses were off and he was smiling, he didn't look terribly sinister at all. He handed Mr. Penguin a business card.

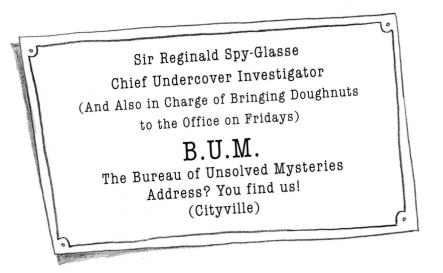

Sir Reginald Spy-Glasse
Chief Undercover Investigator
(And Also in Charge of Bringing Doughnuts to the Office on Fridays)

B.U.M.
The Bureau of Unsolved Mysteries
Address? You find us!
(Cityville)

"The Bureau of Unsolved Mysteries?" said Mr. Penguin. "I've never heard of them!"

"Exactly!" Reginald said, grinning. "You shouldn't have! We are a top-secret organization trying to get to the bottom of strange goings-on and unusual activities! For months now I've been on the hunt for Dr. Veronica Mesmero. We knew she'd traveled to far-flung places, and that huge mirrored panels had appeared on some of the world's greatest monuments. She was definitely up to something, but we didn't know what—except that hypnotism was involved. That's why I've been wearing these special Anti-Hypno specs!"

Mr. Penguin's beak flapped open.

"I've been waiting for a plane to arrive so I could fly over to the fortress and see what was going on over there myself, but you beat me to it. When I saw the hypnotic beam shooting into the sky, I raced over here to see if there was anything I could do to help get you all back, but look—you've already saved the day!"

Mr. Penguin was still concerned. "So you are ABSOLUTELY sure you aren't a baddie?"

Reginald guffawed. "We're like a top secret society of police. We're the good guys! And ladies too, of course!"

Mr. Penguin narrowed his eyes. "But there was a lady at the Golden Pagoda Hotel with these two big bodyguards, and

they were all wearing a badge like yours—
but they weren't up to anything good at
all. They were buying something from a
THIEF!"

Reginald chuckled.

"Ah, yes," he said. "The Enigma
Stone…I'm afraid, Mr. Penguin, you've
got the wrong end of the stick there. The
lady and her two bodyguards are some of
my B.U.M. colleagues: Clara Riddle and
Frank and Trevor Walloppe. They all look
like brutes, don't they? But they're really as
soft and fluffy as cotton candy. You should
see Trevor's collection of crystal unicorns!"

"But they chased us!" said Mr. Penguin.

"We thought YOU were the baddies!"
said Reginald. "The Enigma Stone has

been hidden away in the criminal under-world for decades. Clara was hunting after it for years—she couldn't believe it when it was swiped from under her nose. She sent all the B.U.M. investigators a telegram to be on the lookout for a gang of thieves led by a penguin!"

Reginald guffawed again. "I couldn't believe it when you turned up here! It didn't take me long to realize you weren't a gang of thieves at all, but I didn't get a chance to introduce myself." He paused, then asked, "You do still have the stone?"

Mr. Penguin glanced at Colin, and they both looked sheepish. Very carefully, Mr. Penguin took the enormous diamond from his satchel and put it on the kitchen table. Its sparkles lit up the entire room as he told everyone about how the stone had broken to reveal the gem inside.

Reginald's mouth gaped in shock. "The carvings on the stone were meant to give directions to where the diamond was hidden," he said. "But…"

"It was hidden inside it all along," said Edith, the diamond's light glinting off her specs.

"Well," said Helga, dusting her hands on her apron, "what an exciting few days, and more than one mystery solved. What a clever penguin you are, Mr. Penguin!"

Mr. Penguin went red.

"Well, I couldn't have done it without all of you—my friends!" he said.

As everyone clinked their tea cups together merrily, he glanced around the room and noticed Dr. Mesmero sitting quietly in a corner. In all the kerfuffle, he'd forgotten that she was there. What WERE they going to do with her?

CHAPTER TWENTY-EIGHT

A FRESH START

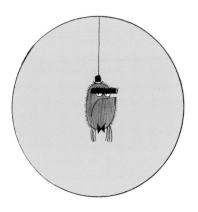

Mr. Penguin asked the question out loud, and everyone turned to look at the strange woman sitting in the shadows.

"Well," said Reginald, "her plan really was *very* dastardly indeed. Taking over the world and controlling everyone in it! We'll take her with us to Cityville, and I'll hand her over to the police with my top-secret report and Dr. Mesmero's notebook."

Mr. Penguin nodded. He supposed that *was* the right thing to do. Dr. Mesmero had been terrifically naughty and caused a lot of dangerous things to happen.

Helga changed the subject by bringing even MORE food to the table, and soon the kitchen was bright and zingy. It felt just like a tea party, except of course it was breakfast time.

But while Mr. Penguin tucked into his second and third helpings of grub, he looked around the room at all the friendly faces and felt a little bit sad.

From reading her notebook, it seemed like Dr. Mesmero never really had a nice happy time like the one he was having now with his friends. Maybe if she had *had* nice friends like Mr. Penguin's, she wouldn't have tried to take over the world? An idea suddenly blossomed in his head. He tapped Reginald Spy-Glasse on the arm with a croissant and explained what he'd just been thinking.

Reginald nodded along thoughtfully, and then said, "So what do you propose to do?"

Mr. Penguin puffed out his chest proudly. It wasn't often that he had very good ideas, but this was definitely one of them! "I am going to hypnotize Dr. Mesmero!" he said.

* * *

Two minutes later, Mr. Penguin was standing on a stool in front of Dr. Mesmero, dangling Colin in front of her face, while everyone else gathered around.

WELL, I THINK THIS IS VERY UN-NECESSARY, said Colin's pad.

"Shhh!" Mr. Penguin hissed. "This is important, Colin! Edith said that *good* hypnotists waggle a pocket watch in front of the person they're hypnotizing. You read it in a library book, didn't you, Edith?"

Edith nodded.

"I don't have a pocket watch," continued Mr. Penguin, "so you'll have to do instead."

Colin popped his pad away, rolled his eyes, and let himself dangle limply on the end of a strand of web.

The room was silent. Mr. Penguin focused on Dr. Mesmero's eyes and the faint swirls in her pupils. He took a deep breath and said in his nice telephone voice, "Dr. Veronica Mesmero, you no longer remember your old life as a mad doctor-inventor-hypnotist. You have *no* plans *ever* to take over the world. All you remember is a happy life here on the mountain. You will now help Dieter train Colonel Tuftybum for the next Rodent Games, and you will use your clever engineering skills to help Lisle fix and look after the von Clonker clock. You will be happy, and kind, and…"

Mr. Penguin thought for a moment, then continued, "And you will always make sure there's a jar of fish paste in the pantry. You will wake from your trance when I clap my flippers."

Mr. Penguin lowered Colin's web and slapped his flippers together.

Everyone watched intently, but Dr. Mesmero just sat there. Then suddenly she blinked, shook her head, and yawned.

"Goodness!" she said in a sparkly voice. "I must have nodded off for a moment. It's so cozy and warm in here!"

She looked around at everyone and smiled. It wasn't a snarly sort of grin like in the fortress, but a lovely, friendly smile. "Ooh!" she cried. "A party! I'd have brought some fish paste sandwiches if I'd known!"

Mr. Penguin beamed. His plan had worked!

CHAPTER TWENTY-NINE

HOME?

The plane Reginald had ordered didn't arrive until the sun was starting to bob down behind the mountains, painting everything orangey-pink. It was a bit of a battered old thing—a cargo plane, like the one Edith had "borrowed," but not *quite* as ropey. The pilot was another undercover B.U.M. agent. She was a bit disappointed to find out she wouldn't be flying on a daring rescue mission, but she cheered up when Mr. Penguin gave her his best beaky grin.

Earlier, while they'd waited for the plane, Mr. Penguin and the gang had enjoyed the village of Schneedorf-on-the-Peak without having to worry about dangerous missions or sneaky, sinister people creeping around corners. And the new Dr. Mesmero had turned out to be an absolute hoot! After she'd spent a couple of hours poring over the ancient blueprints for the von Clonker clock with Lisle, she'd insisted that everyone join her outside to build a snowman.

Mr. Penguin hadn't been keen on the idea at first. He was extremely busy sitting by the warm oven, wrapped up in a pile of blankets with his eyes closed while his feet soaked in a bowl of warm, soapy water. But once he was dragged outside he'd really enjoyed himself.

The snowman building had turned into a snowball fight, and then that had turned into a new game called "Oh Where Has Gordon Gone? Really Mr. Penguin, You Must Be Careful With Your Snowballs."

Gordon had been found safe and well and was soon happily back on Edith's head. You could never tell with Gordon because he was always so brave in the face of Mild Peril and Absolute Danger, but Mr. Penguin thought his friend seemed glad to be out of his hamster costume and back in the bobble hat Helga had given him.

When the plane arrived and it was time to board, Mr. Penguin felt a bit muddled.

He was, of course, very excited to get back to Cityville—his cozy igloo was waiting for him, as was the Popular Plaice 24-Hour Diner with its never-ending supply of fish finger sandwiches. But he did feel a bit sad to be leaving his new friends.

Lisle, Dieter, Helga, and Dr. Mesmero (now she wasn't trying to take over the world) had been so nice to the Adventurers.

"I promise we'll soon be back," Mr. Penguin said, just before he waddled onto the plane. "But this time for a vacation!"

Helga handed him a great hamper of food for the journey. "Promise?" she said.

Mr. Penguin nodded. "On my last fish finger sandwich!"

* * *

A few minutes later, the plane was soaring above the clouds toward Cityville. In the back, Edith and Gordon were already dozing. Colin was upside down, fast asleep, while holding up his notepad, which said:

ZZZZZzzzzzz

But Mr. Penguin couldn't get comfortable. Despite the yummy picnic from Helga, his stomach was still grumbling. He knew what would stop it rumbling, but *of course,* up in the air there wasn't a fish finger sandwich to be found. Just a load of cardboard boxes on their way to the shops of Cityville.

WAIT A MINUTE! What was that? Mr. Penguin scanned back over the labels.

Walter Trout's Luxury Fish Paste! Could…

could it be true? An entire box of fish paste here on the plane?

He knew it was naughty, but his flippers had a mind of their own, and he found himself ripping open the box.

He gasped. Inside there was jar after jar of the stuff just waiting to be gobbled up. Surely whoever it was for wouldn't mind him having one or two?

Mr. Penguin popped open one of the lids and stuck his entire beak into the jar. It was scrumptious! It was delicious! It was…

He heard someone clearing their throat politely. Mr. Penguin turned to find Reginald Spy-Glasse standing in the

door to the cockpit. Behind him, the pilot was fiddling with some dials.

"Bit of a change of plan, old chap." Reginald said, trying not to stare at the jar stuck on Mr. Penguin's beak. "A message just came through for you on the radio. Someone is requesting your help with an Urgent Matter. We're going to have to divert the plane."

Mr. Penguin sighed.

His fish finger sandwich at the diner in Cityville would have to wait. Another exciting adventure was calling.

THE END

(Until the next, next time!)

A BRIEF HISTORY OF THE B.U.M.

The Bureau of Unsolved Mysteries (B.U.M.) is a Top Secret organization with operatives working across the globe.

Created in 1810 by Archduke Herbert Spy-Glasse after he lost his glasses, the organization quickly grew and began to investigate many strange and perplexing mysteries.

Originally based in Londontown, B.U.M. is now believed to be based across the pond in Cityville, where it is headed up by one of Herbert's descendants, Sir Reginald Spy-Glasse.

B.U.M. members can often only be picked out by the distinctive badge they wear based on the company's logo—a bejeweled eye set within a bronze magnifying glass with a piece of shiny black stone forming a stylized question mark.

The Cityville Times

MORNING EDITION — 30th NOVEMBER

VON CLONKER CLOCK GETS A FACE LIFT!

Work begins today in the far off, northerly village of Schneedorf-on-the-Peak, giving the famous antique town clock—The King Ludvig von Clonker Memorial Clock—a much needed repair and overhaul.

Dr. Veronica Mesmero, a whiz with anything clockwork and who is helping with the repairs said: "My young colleague Lisle Strudel and I will be giving the clock a thorough once-over to make sure it is in tip-top condition, as well as building a new clockwork cuckoo using the original blueprints to guide us."

The mechanics expert then went on to offer this reporter several delicious fish paste sandwiches she had made herself in the local bakery where she works part-time.

Full story with clock diagrams on page 7

WHAT AN ENIGMA!

MYSTERIOUS LOST GEM RETURNS TO THE CITY!

Visit THE PYRAMIDS

LUXURY HOLIDAYS on PAGE 15

There were celebrations today at the Cityville University's School of Archaeology when local Adventurer (and penguin), Mr. Penguin, delivered a famous (and long thought lost forever) diamond to Professor Stout-Girdle, the school's principal.

Mr. Penguin and his associates, Colin, Edith Hedge, and Gordon had been tasked several months ago with tracking the Enigma Stone by Professor Stout-Girdle, but the group of Adventurers and the university soon discovered there was even more of an enigma around the object than anyone had first thought!

For decades, the Enigma Stone was believed to have been an ancient carved rock. The message written on it, once translated, would, it was said, point to the location of a gigantic, flawless diamond. However, following quite an adventure that Mr. Penguin was far too humble to tell to the press at the handing over ceremony, the local group of Adventurers discovered that the diamond had been hidden inside the Enigma Stone all along.

A beaming Professor Stout-Girdle said at the ceremony, "This is a great day both for the university and Cityville and I have Mr. Penguin and his friends to thank for bringing this priceless diamond home where it can be fully examined and its secrets unravelled."

She added, "I am more than delighted to hand over Mr. Penguin's reward for solving this rather tricky case."

There had been some delay in the delivery of the diamond back to the university when Mr. Penguin and his band of Adventurers' plane broke down on a mountain far from Cityville in some very inclement weather. However, the gang sat out the blizzards and said absolutely nothing exciting or noteworthy or dangerous occurred during this time.

Full story page 3

MR. PENGUIN'S

NEXT ADVENTURE IS COMING SOON

PRAISE FOR MR. PENGUIN AND THE LOST TREASURE

★ "Lighthearted and humorous…
The short chapters and riotous plot
will easily win this series starter fans."
—*Booklist*

"A surprising, twisting, and dangerous
quest. The plot is full of turns…
Mr. Penguin is delightful."
—*Foreword Reviews*

"Sure to pull readers along."
—*Kirkus Reviews*

"Fresh and funny."
—*School Library Journal*